U0033926

新制多益

聽力 搶分訓練營

3 STEPS 打造 高效聽力腦

解題技巧練習本

作者 Park Hye-young / Jeon Ji-won / Joseph Bazil Manietta　　譯者 關亭薇 / 蔡裴驊 / 蘇裕承

MP3
寂天雲 APP

如何下載 MP3 音檔

❶ 寂天雲 APP 聆聽：掃描書上 QR Code 下載「寂天雲 – 英日語學習隨身聽」APP。加入會員後，用 APP 內建掃描器再次掃描書上 QR Code，即可使用 APP 聆聽音檔。

❷ 官網下載音檔：請上「寂天閱讀網」（www.icosmos.com.tw），註冊會員／登入後，搜尋本書，進入本書頁面，點選「MP3 下載」下載音檔，存於電腦等其他播放器聆聽使用。

新制多益
聽力 搶分訓練營

3 STEPS 打造高效聽力腦　解題技巧練習本 ＋ 中譯解析本

作 者 Park Hye-young / Jeon Ji-won / Joseph Bazil Manietta

譯 者 關亭薇／蔡裴驊／蘇裕承

編 輯 張盛傑

校 對 黃詩韻／許嘉華

主 編 丁宥暄

內頁排版 蔡怡柔

封面設計 林書玉

製程管理 洪巧玲

發 行 人 黃朝萍

出 版 者 寂天文化事業股份有限公司

電 話 +886-(0)2-2365-9739

傳 真 +886-(0)2-2365-9835

網 址 www.icosmos.com.tw

讀者服務 onlineservice@icosmos.com.tw

出版日期 2024 年 4 月初版再刷 （寂天雲隨身聽 APP 版） (0103)

토익 부스터 LC

Copyright © 2019 by Park Hye-young & Jeon Ji-won & Joseph Bazil Manietta

All rights reserved.

Traditional Chinese translation copyright © 2020 by Cosmos Culture Ltd.

This Traditional Chinese edition was published by arrangement with Darakwon, Inc.

through Agency Liang

版權所有　請勿翻印

郵撥帳號 1998620-0 寂天文化事業股份有限公司

訂書金額未滿 1000 元，請外加運費 100 元。

〔若有破損，請寄回更換，謝謝。〕

新制多益聽力搶分訓練營：3 STEPS 打造高效聽力腦 （寂
天雲隨身聽 APP 版）/Park Hye-young, Jeon Ji-won,
Joseph Bazil Manietta 著；關亭薇，蔡裴驊，蘇裕承譯 . --
初版 . -- [臺北市]：
寂天文化, 2022.08
　　面；　公分
ISBN 978-626-300-149-7 (16K 平裝)

1. 多益測驗

805.1895

作者序

「新制多益要怎麼準備才好呢？」

　　多益測驗改制後，我們最常從學生口中聽到的話，就是「多益突然變得好難」。同時，我們也看到不少學生讀完基礎教材後，在準備練習坊間出版的多益模擬題庫之時，就因為龐大的內容頓時頭昏眼花，甚至就此放棄。有鑑於此情況，我們為已經打下多益基礎，卻仍舊對準備多益測驗無所適從的學生們編寫了這本書。只要讀完本書，原本令你感到茫然的多益測驗，將能變得得心應手。

本書的特色如下：

- 每個 Unit 均列出多益聽力測驗常考的核心單字、片語及句型，讓學習者背誦、練習。

- 囊括多種練習題，讓學習者能由淺入深逐步掌握各種題型，並預先進行實戰演練。

- 不光只是練習測驗試題，本書還將各篇章的試題彙整成一個大題，讓學習者練習聽寫，進行扎實的聽力訓練。

- 最後附上一回 50 題的 Half Test，讓學習者在學完所有聽力測驗的重點後，能夠透過模擬測驗來檢測自己的實力進步多少。

Park, Hye-young
Jeon, Ji-won

本書特色

PART 1 照片描述（4 UNITS）

STEP 1 題型演練

看照片、聽音檔，並選出例題的答案。
作答完畢後，再研究「解題重點」，確
實掌握該考題類型的要點。接著，做
做看與同一張照片有關的是非題，再
次複習與該題型相關的句型用法。

STEP 2 常考用法

彙整出該題型中的高頻用法。再做下
面的「STEP 3 聽寫練習」，看看這些
用法是如何實際應用在題目裡的。

STEP 3 聽寫練習

請先做做看練習題，再次熟悉該題型。
接著，請再聽一次音檔做聽寫練習，
確實吸收相關用法，將其內化成自己
的知識。

PART 2 應答問題（9 UNITS）

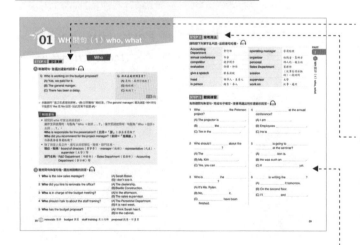

STEP 1 題型演練

練習該類題型的例題後，研究「解題
重點」中所列出的解題關鍵，當中還
會舉出各種問句和答句，讓你瞬間理
解要點。

STEP 2 常考用法

彙整出該題型中的高頻單字和片語。
與 PART 1 的學習方式相同，下方的
「STEP 3 聽寫練習」將讓你了解這些
單字片語是如何實際應用在題目裡的。

STEP 3 聽寫練習

做做看六道練習題，再次熟悉該題型
的學習重點。接著，請再聽一次音檔
做聽寫練習，重覆統整該題型的重點
和相關用法。

PART 3 簡短對話（8 UNITS）・ PART 4 簡短獨白（7 UNITS）

STEP 1 題型演練

聽完簡短的對話或獨白後，選出正確答案，藉此熟悉各種考題的類型。接著，研究完「解題重點」後，再聽一次對話或獨白，完成下面補充的練習題。

STEP 2 常考用法

彙整出該題型中的高頻單字、片語和句型。有別於 PART 1、PART 2 的學習方式，下方的 B 大題將直接套用這些單字和用法，請練習聽寫完成句子填空。

STEP 3 聽寫練習

請先聆聽兩篇對話或獨白，選出正確答案。接著，再聽一次對話或獨白做聽寫練習，重覆統整該題型的重點和相關用法。

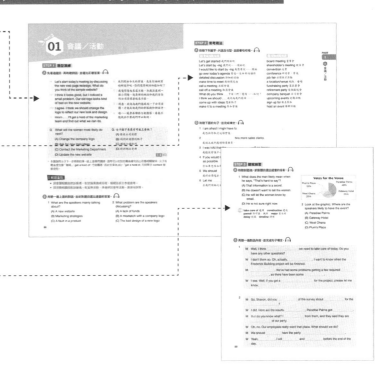

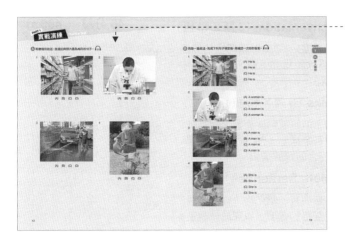

實戰演練

本書共有 28 個 UNIT，在每一個 UNIT 最後，附上「實戰演練」試題，讓你以與實際測驗相同的模擬試題進行實戰演練，再次統整學習過的內容。作答完畢後，請再聽一次音檔做聽寫練習，確實吸收相關用法，將其內化變成自己的知識。

Half Test

學完本書的所有內容後，請做做看書末所附的 50 題聽力模擬測驗，測試看看自己學到了多少。

關於新制多益（NEW TOEIC）

新制多益是什麼呢？

TOEIC（多益）為 Test of English for International Communication（國際溝通英語測驗）的縮寫，針對英語非母語人士所設計，測驗其在國際環境中生活或執行工作時所具備的英語應用能力。2018 年 3 月起，改版的多益測驗——**NEW TOEIC**（**新制多益**）在台灣正式上路。測驗分數被廣泛作為人才招募、升遷、外派海外者等各項選拔之依據。

題型介紹

新制多益分為**聽力閱讀測驗**（**Listening & Reading Test**）及**口說寫作測驗**（**Speaking & Writing Test**）。**聽力閱讀測驗**為紙筆測驗，共 200 題單選題，測驗時間為 120 分鐘。聽力與閱讀兩者分開計時。

題型	PART	內容	題數	時間	分數
聽力測驗 Listening Comprehension	1	**照片描述 Picture Description** 一邊看試題冊上的照片，一邊聆聽錄音播放的四個選項，並從中選出最符合照片內容的選項。	6	45 分鐘	495 分
	2	**應答問題 Questions & Responses** 聆聽錄音播放的疑問句或直述句，以及對應的三個回答句或回應句，並從中選出最符合問答邏輯的選項。	25		
	3	**簡短對話 Short Conversations**（3 題 X 13 組） 聆聽兩人對話或三人對話，閱讀試題冊上的問題及四個答案選項（部分題組亦有圖表），並從中選出最符合問題的選項。	39		
	4	**簡短獨白 Short Talks**（3 題 X 10 組） 聆聽一段廣播、公告、演說或新聞報導，閱讀試題冊上的問題及四個答案選項（部分題組亦有圖表），並從中選出最符合問題的選項。	30		
閱讀測驗 Reading Comprehension	5	**單句填空 Incomplete Sentences** 閱讀一個英文句子，句中有一處空格，從四個選項中選出一個最符合空格的選項，以完成一個正確、完整的句子。	30	75 分鐘	495 分
	6	**短文填空 Text Completion**（4 題 X 4 篇） 閱讀一篇短文，內容可能是一篇電子郵件、一篇廣告或是一份說明書，當中會有四處空格（4 題），然後從每一題的四個選項中選出一個最適合填入空格的單字、片語或句子。	16		
	7	**閱讀測驗 Reading Passages** （單篇閱讀 29 題＋多篇閱讀 25 題） 單篇閱讀為一篇文章搭配 2 到 4 個問題，多篇文章則為兩篇或三篇有關聯性的文章搭配 5 個問題。文章內容可能是廣告、報紙上的報導、商業文件或公告。	54		
	TOTAL		200	120 分鐘	990 分

命題方向

多益測驗考的是在日常生活和執行工作時所需的英語能力，因此考題也針對這兩大範圍出題。當中與商業有關的內容並不會涉及專業知識，同時也不會針對特定國家或文化出題。詳細的命題範圍如下：

一般商務（General Business）	簽約、協商、行銷、業務、企劃、會談
辦公場所（Office）	會議、信件、通知、電話、傳真、電子郵件、辦公室設備與用具
人事（Personnel）	求職、招聘、升遷、退休、支薪、獎金
財務（Finance and Budgeting）	投資、稅金、會計、銀行業務
生產（Manufacturing）	製造、工廠營運、品管
開發（Corporate Development）	研究調查、實驗、新品開發
採購（Purchasing）	購物、訂購、估價、結算
外食（Dining Out）	午餐、晚餐、聚餐、餐敘活動
健康（Health）	醫院、診斷、醫療保險
旅遊（Travel）	交通工具、住宿、車站與機場指南、預約與取消
娛樂（Entertainment）	電影、表演、音樂、美術、展覽
住宅／企業房產（Housing / Corporate Property）	建設、不動產買賣與租賃、電力與瓦斯相關服務

多益成績與英語能力對照

多益成績	英語能力	證書顏色
905-990 分	英文能力已十分近似英語母語人士，能夠流暢有條理地表達意見、參與對話、主持英文會議、調和衝突並做出結論，語言使用上即使有瑕疵，亦不會造成理解上的困擾。	金色（860-990）
785-900 分	可有效運用英語滿足社交及工作所需、措辭恰當、表達流暢；但在某些特定情形下，如面臨緊張壓力、討論話題過於冷僻艱澀時，仍會顯現出語言能力不足的狀況。	藍色（730-855）
605-780 分	可以用英語進行一般社交場合的談話，能夠應付例行性的業務需求，參加英文會議，聽取大部分要點；但無法流利的以英文發表意見、作辯論，使用的字彙、句型亦以一般常見者為主。	綠色（470-725）
405-600 分	英文文字溝通能力尚可、會話方面稍嫌詞彙不足、語句簡單，但已能掌握少量工作相關語言，可以從事英語相關程度較低的工作。	棕色（220-465）
255-400 分	語言能力僅僅侷限在簡單的一般日常生活對話，同時無法做連續性交談，亦無法用英文工作。	
10-250 分	只能以背誦的句子進行問答而不能自行造句，尚無法將英語當作溝通工具來使用。	橘色（10-215）

目 錄 Contents

別冊：中譯解析本

PART 1

照片描述
Picture Description

01 單人獨照

A 聆聽下列敘述，並選出與照片最為相符的句子。🎧 001

(A) A woman is wearing a scarf.
一名女子圍著圍巾。

(B) A woman is repairing a copy machine.
一名女子正在修理影印機。

(C) A woman is making a copy.
一名女子正在影印。

(D) A woman is working on a computer.
一名女子正在用電腦工作。

答案 (C)

▶ 照片中的女子正在「影印」，應選出正確描寫該動作的選項。「make a copy」（影印）的現在進行式為「is making a copy」（正在影印），故正確答案為 (C)。

📖 解題重點

- PART 1 中最常使用的時態是現在進行式，請務必熟悉它的用法：「**be 動詞＋ V-ing**」。它用於表達眼前所發生的事，因此最適合用來描述人物的動作或狀態。
- 只要聽到照片裡沒有的東西，該選項便不是答案。陷阱選項經常會用到與照片有關、但未出現在照片中的單字，讓人產生混淆。
- 答案也有可能是針對背景或周遭事物做描述的選項。雖然照片以人物為主，但描寫背景或人物周邊事物的選項也有可能是答案。

B 聆聽下列句子，與上面照片相符的內容選 **O**，不相符的選 **X**。🎧 002

1 A woman **is wearing** business attire.   (○) (×)

2 A woman **is putting on** a jacket.   (○) (×)

3 A woman is using **a fax machine**.   (○) (×)

4 A woman **is pressing** a button on a copy machine.   (○) (×)

5 A woman **is standing in front of some office equipment**.   (○) (×)

6 The copy machine has **a paper jam**.   (○) (×)

7 **Books are stacked** on the floor.   (○) (×)

字彙 **business attire** 正式套裝　**equipment** 設備　**paper jam** 卡紙　**stack** 堆疊

STEP 2　常考用法

請聆聽下列與人物動作有關的用法，並跟著唸唸看。 🎧 003

1 描述人物的手腳動作

be passing out copies 正在分發影印文件
be hanging a picture 正在掛一幅畫
be crossing an intersection 正穿越十字路口
be boarding a boat 正登上一艘船
be walking along the beach 正沿著海灘走
be raising one's hand （某人）正舉起手
be walking under an archway 正走在拱門下
be reaching for a cell phone 正伸手拿行動電話
be strolling along the river 正沿著河邊漫步

2 描述人物的外表或狀態

be sitting in a waiting room
正坐在等候室（候診室、候車室等）裡
be lying on the grass 正躺在草地上
be leaning against a wall 正靠著牆壁
be holding merchandise 正拿著貨品
be trying on a bracelet
正在試戴一條手鍊／一個手鐲
be taking off a coat 正脫下外套／大衣

3 描述人物做事的動作

be putting up a tent 正在搭帳蓬
be rearranging chairs 正在重排椅子
be putting away a microscope
正把顯微鏡放回原位
be setting the table 正在擺餐桌
be assembling furniture 正在組裝家具
be watering a plant 正給一株植物澆水
be placing books on a shelf 正把書放在架子上
be stacking dishes 正把盤子疊起來
be clearing off a kitchen table
正在清理廚房餐桌

4 描述人物的視線

be looking in a drawer 正在查看抽屜裡面
be examining safety glasses 正在檢查護目鏡
be staring at a document 正盯著一份文件看
be checking one's watch
（某人）正在查看手錶
be studying the menu 正仔細看菜單
be reviewing papers 正在審閱文件

STEP 3　聽寫練習

聆聽下列敘述，並選出所有與照片相符的句子。接著請再聽一遍敘述，並完成句子填空。 🎧 004

1

(A) A man is _____ a _____ .

(B) A man is _____ a _____ .

(C) A man is _____ a computer screen.

(D) A man is _____ a desk.

2

(A) She is _____ in the kitchen.

(B) She is _____ a pair of _____ .

(C) She is _____ an apron.

(D) She is _____ a tray.

實戰演練 Practice Test

A 聆聽題目敘述，並選出與照片最為相符的句子。 🎧 005

1

(A) (B) (C) (D)

2

(A) (B) (C) (D)

3

(A) (B) (C) (D)

4

(A) (B) (C) (D)

B 再聽一遍敘述，完成下列句子填空後，再確認一次你的答案。 🎧006

1

(A) He is _____.

(B) He is _____.

(C) He is _____.

(D) He is _____.

2

(A) A woman is _____.

(B) A woman is _____.

(C) A woman is _____.

(D) A woman is _____.

3

(A) A man is _____.

(B) A man is _____.

(C) A man is _____.

(D) A man is _____.

4

(A) She is _____.

(B) She is _____.

(C) She is _____.

(D) She is _____.

02 雙人照片／多人照片

Ⓐ 聆聽下列敘述，並選出與照片最為相符的句子。🎧007

(A) The women are shaking hands.
這些女子正在握手。

(B) One of the women is wearing a scarf.
其中一名女子圍著圍巾。

(C) They are working on a project.
她們正在處理一個專案。

(D) One of the women has her hand on her hair.
其中一名女子把手放在頭髮上。

答案 (A)

▶ 應選出描寫兩人同時做出的動作之選項。(A) 的「are shaking hands」為「shake hands」的現在進行式，表示「握手」，故為正確答案。

🕮 解題重點

- 聆聽時，請將焦點放在兩人同時做出的動作上。快速掌握兩人同時做出的動作，並專心聆聽是否出現相符的敘述。

- 仔細聆聽句子的主詞。注意選項中的主詞為「one of them」、「some people」，還是「they」、「the man」或「both」，藉此分辨該敘述是針對照片裡的其中一人，還是某一部分的人。

- 先想一下描述人物動作或狀態的用法。在聆聽錄音前，請先想想有哪些用法與照片人物的動作或狀態有關。

Ⓑ 聆聽下列句子，與上面照片相符的內容選 O，不相符的選 X。🎧008

1 One of the women is **holding a file**. （ O ）（ × ）

2 They are **smiling at each other**. （ O ）（ × ）

3 The women are **having a conference call**. （ O ）（ × ）

4 **Both of them** are wearing **formal clothes**. （ O ）（ × ）

5 **They are seated** right next to each other. （ O ）（ × ）

6 A woman is **taking notes out of** her pocket. （ O ）（ × ）

7 **The women** are sitting **across from each other**. （ O ）（ × ）

字彙 **have a conference call** 開視訊會議　**formal clothes** 正式服裝　**be seated** 坐、就座
across from 在……的對面

STEP 2　常考用法

請聆聽下列與人物動作有關的用法，並跟著唸唸看。 🎧009

① 描述人物的動作

be shaking hands 正在握手
be greeting each other 正彼此打招呼
be smiling at each other 正彼此對著對方微笑
be talking on the phone 正在講電話
be working on the computer 正在用電腦工作
be packing up boxes 正在裝箱
be stacking boxes 正把箱子堆疊起來
be mopping the floor 正在拖地

② 描述人物的外表或狀態

be wearing uniforms 穿著制服
be wearing a tie 打著領帶
be wearing glasses 戴著眼鏡
be putting on a pair of shoes 正穿上一雙鞋子
be buttoning a coat 正在扣外套的扣子
be taking off their shoes （他們）正在脫鞋子

③ 描述人物的視線

be staring at the screen 正盯著螢幕看
be looking at some figures 正在看著一些數字
be watching a performance 正在看一場表演
be looking out the window 正看著窗外
be looking at the bulletin board 正看著布告欄
be going over some documents
正在仔細查看一些文件
be reviewing a document 正在審閱一份文件
be examining a machine 正在檢查一台機器
be studying the menu 正在細看菜單

④ 描述人物的姿勢

be seated around the table 圍著桌子而坐
be standing at the counter 正站在櫃台前面
be jogging along the river 正沿著河邊慢跑
be holding onto the railing 正抓著欄杆
be bending over to pick up something
正在俯身拾起某物

STEP 3　聽寫練習

聆聽下列敘述，並選出所有與照片相符的句子。接著請再聽一遍敘述，並完成句子填空。 010

1

(A) The people are _____ the
_____.

(B) They are _____.

(C) Some people are _____.

(D) The _____ is _____ now.

2

(A) They are _____ in a _____.

(B) They are _____.

(C) They are _____ on the shelf.

(D) They are _____.

Ⓐ 聆聽題目敘述，並選出與照片最為相符的句子。 🎧 011

1

(A)　(B)　(C)　(D)

2

(A)　(B)　(C)　(D)

3

(A)　(B)　(C)　(D)

4

(A)　(B)　(C)　(D)

B 再聽一遍敘述，完成下列句子填空後，再確認一次你的答案。 🎧 012

1

(A) The men _____.

(B) The men _____.

(C) They _____.

(D) They _____.

2

(A) They _____.

(B) A man _____.

(C) A woman _____.

(D) They _____.

3

(A) The men _____.

(B) They _____.

(C) They _____.

(D) One of the men _____.

4

(A) The people _____.

(B) One of the people _____.

(C) Both of them _____.

(D) The man _____.

03 描述事物的照片

Ⓐ 聆聽下列敘述，並選出與照片最為相符的句子。🎧013

(A) Drinks have been left on a table.
飲料留在桌上。

(B) A sitting area is lit up by lamps.
休息區點著燈。

(C) The armchairs are being cleaned.
（某人）正在清潔扶手椅。

(D) Cushions have been placed on a sofa.
沙發上放著靠墊。

答案 (B)

▶ 應選出正確描寫照片裡事物的選項。(B) 使用被動語態，描寫燈具點亮了休息區，故為正確答案。若聽到像 (C) 當中的現在進行式被動語態時，請務必確認是否為針對人物動作的描述。

解題重點

- 請記住被動語態的用法。描寫事物的位置或狀態時，可用現在式的被動語態：「is/are + p.p.」，和現在完成式的被動語態：「have/has + been + p.p.」。
- 若選項中出現 being，通常是針對人物的描述。現在進行式被動語態「is/are + being + p.p.」指的是「某動作正在被（某人）執行／（某人）正在執行某動作」。因此，若聽到選項中有使用現在進行式被動語態，請注意該句子描述的是否為人物動作。

Ⓑ 聆聽下列句子，與上面照片相符的內容選 O，不相符的選 X。🎧014

1 Flowers **have been left** on a table. （ ○ ）（ × ）

2 Lamps **have been turned on** in the room. （ ○ ）（ × ）

3 Refreshments **have been placed** on a table. （ ○ ）（ × ）

4 Flowers **are being arranged** in a vase. （ ○ ）（ × ）

5 The sofa is facing **the clock**. （ ○ ）（ × ）

6 **Workers** are vacuuming the carpet. （ ○ ）（ × ）

7 Refreshments **are being served**. （ ○ ）（ × ）

字彙 **turn on** 打開（電器）　**refreshment** 茶點、便餐　**vase** 花瓶　**face** 面向……、正對……
vacuum 用吸塵器清掃

STEP 2　常考用法

請聆聽下列與事物描述有關的用法，並跟著唸唸看。 015

1 商店、倉庫

Containers are stacked up on the floor.
容器堆放在地板上。

Some boxes are lined up in a warehouse.
倉庫裡放著一排一排的盒子。

Some vegetables have been placed in a shopping cart.
一些蔬菜放在購物車裡。

Merchandise has been displayed.
貨物已被陳列出來。

Some shelves are being assembled.
（某人）正在組裝一些貨架。

Groceries are being scanned.
（某人）正在掃描一些食品雜貨。

2 花、植物、庭院

There is a vase on the table.
桌上有一個花瓶。

There are potted plants in the garden.
花園裡有盆栽。

Flowers have been arranged in vases.
花瓶裡插著花。

Trees have been planted in a garden.
花園裡種著樹。

Plants are being watered.
（某人）正在給植物澆水。

A picnic table is being cleared off.
（某人）正在將野餐餐桌搬開。

3 辦公室用品、實驗室器具

A microscope has been placed on a table.
桌上放著一台顯微鏡。

A whiteboard is propped against a door.
一面白板靠著門。

A printer has been stored in a box.
一台印表機收在箱子裡。

Binoculars have been left on a table.
桌上留有雙筒望遠鏡。

Some laboratory equipment is being moved.
（某人）正在搬動一些實驗室的設備。

Some objects are being examined.
（某人）正在檢查一些物品。

4 客廳、書房、廚房

A framed picture is facing the sofa.
沙發對面有一幅裱框的畫。

Books are piled on a desk.
書桌上堆放著書。

Some furniture is being rearranged.
（某人）正在重新排列一些家具。

The kitchen is being mopped.
（某人）正在拖廚房地板。

Chairs are being stacked.
（某人）正在把椅子疊起來。

Food is being removed from an oven.
（某人）正從烤箱裡拿出食物。

STEP 3　聽寫練習

聆聽下列敘述，並選出所有與照片相符的句子。接著請再聽一遍敘述，並完成句子填空。 016

1

(A) A laptop _____ _____.

(B) Some books _____ on the floor.

(C) A potted plant _____ on the table.

(D) Glasses _____ next to a cell phone.

2

(A) Groceries _____ in a cart.

(B) Fruit is _____ in a store.

(C) A customer _____ some fruit on a scale.

(D) Some food _____ into a basket.

實戰演練 Practice Test

Ⓐ 聆聽題目敘述，並選出與照片最為相符的句子。 🎧 017

1

(A)   (B)   (C)   (D)

2

(A)   (B)   (C)   (D)

3

(A)   (B)   (C)   (D)

4

(A)   (B)   (C)   (D)

B 再聽一遍敘述，完成下列句子填空後，再確認一次你的答案。 018

1

(A) _____ in the park.

(B) A picnic basket _____ on the grass.

(C) A gardener is _____ .

(D) Dishes _____ .

2

(A) Kitchen pots _____ on the stove.

(B) Vegetables _____ .

(C) Dishes _____ on the countertop.

(D) _____ a knife on the chopping board.

3

(A) Office equipment _____ .

(B) A microscope _____ on the table.

(C) A round table _____ in the room.

(D) Lights _____ on the ceiling.

4

(A) _____ at a cash register.

(B) Products _____ on the shelves.

(C) A clerk _____ the shelves with cans.

(D) A shopping cart _____ with groceries.

04 描述背景的照片

Ⓐ 聆聽下列敘述，並選出與照片最為相符的句子。 🎧019

(A) A house is being built.
（某人）正在蓋一間房子。

(B) There are some trees near a house.
靠近房子的地方有一些樹。

(C) The houses have been renovated.
房子整修過了。

(D) Snow is being cleaned.
（某人）正在掃雪。

答案 (B)

▶ (B) 描寫房子周邊的景象，故為正確答案。(A) 和 (D) 使用現在進行式被動語態（is/are ＋ being ＋ p.p.），為針對人物動作的描述。

💡 解題重點

- 請記住「There is/are ＋名詞」的用法。描寫事物的位置或狀態時，可用「There is/are ＋名詞」，表示「有……」。
  There is a flowerpot in front of the house. 房子前面有一個花盆。
  There are some cars traveling along the river. 有一些車子正沿著河邊行駛。

- 描寫背景或風景時，經常使用「be 動詞＋介系詞片語」。
  The logs are under the table. 桌子底下有木材。
  Some paintings are on the shelf. 架子上有一些畫作。

Ⓑ 聆聽下列句子，與上面照片相符的內容選 O，不相符的選 X。 🎧020

1 The ground **is covered with** snow. 　　　　　　　　（ ○ ）（ × ）

2 Some trees **have been planted** near the house. 　　　（ ○ ）（ × ）

3 The house **is being cleaned**. 　　　　　　　　　　（ ○ ）（ × ）

4 Snow **has been cleaned** away. 　　　　　　　　　　（ ○ ）（ × ）

5 **There are** some trees **between the two houses**. 　　（ ○ ）（ × ）

6 All of the windows **are open**. 　　　　　　　　　　（ ○ ）（ × ）

7 The windows **are being wiped**. 　　　　　　　　　　（ ○ ）（ × ）

字彙 be covered with 覆蓋著……、蓋滿……　plant 栽種　clean away 清除　wipe 擦拭

STEP 2　常考用法

請聆聽下列與背景及風景描述有關的用法，並跟著唸唸看。🎧021

1 描述車輛或道路

Cars are running on the road.
車子正在馬路上行駛。

Vehicles are traveling in both directions.
雙向都有車子在行駛。

Cars are parked along the street.
車子沿著街道停放。

There are lampposts alongside the road.
沿著馬路邊有路燈柱。

2 描述房子或建築物周邊

A car has been parked in the driveway.
一輛車子停在車道上。

The roof of the house is being fixed.
（某人）正在修理這棟房子的屋頂。

Plants have been placed in front of the house.
房子前面擺放著植物。

There is a flowerpot near the door.
靠近門的地方有一個花盆。

3 描述森林、大自然、公園

Trees have been planted along the road.
樹木沿著道路種植。

There are some benches in the park.
公園裡有一些長椅。

Boats are docked in a harbor.
船隻停放在港口內。

Boats are sailing in the sea.
船正在海中航行。

There is a bridge over the river.
河上有一座橋。

Trees are reflected in the water.
樹木倒映在水中。

A path winds through the woods.
一條小徑蜿蜒穿過樹林。

Mountains can be seen in the distance.
可以看到遠方的山脈。

A monument overlooks the pathway.
一座紀念碑俯瞰著小路。

STEP 3　聽寫練習

聆聽下列敘述，並選出所有與照片相符的句子。接著請再聽一遍敘述，並完成句子填空。🎧022

1

(A) A boat _____ in a _____.

(B) There is a _____ the _____.

(C) The boat is _____.

(D) _____ over the water.

2

(A) Some cars _____ in the
_____.

(B) There is a _____.

(C) There is _____ the house.

(D) The road _____ the house.

A 聆聽題目敘述,並選出與照片最為相符的句子。 🎧023

1

(A) (B) (C) (D)

2

(A) (B) (C) (D)

3

(A) (B) (C) (D)

4

(A) (B) (C) (D)

B 再聽一遍敘述，完成下列句子填空後，再確認一次你的答案。 024

1

(A) _____ at the traffic light.

(B) _____ in both directions.

(C) The buildings _____.

(D) Some cars _____.

2

(A) The trees _____.

(B) A _____ the woods.

(C) A hiking trail _____.

(D) The road _____.

3

(A) There are shelves _____.

(B) The garage _____.

(C) The tires _____ away.

(D) _____ scattered on the floor.

4

(A) _____ in the sky.

(B) Some people _____.

(C) _____ the square.

(D) The gate is _____.

A 選出正確的中文意思。

1　cross an intersection　　　(A) 穿越十字路口　　(B) 指揮交通
2　mow the lawn　　　　　　(A) 清掃庭院　　　　(B) 除草坪的草
3　lean against the bench　　　(A) 清潔長椅　　　　(B) 靠著長椅
4　arrange flowers　　　　　(A) 插花　　　　　　(B) 買花
5　renovate the house　　　　(A) 破壞房子　　　　(B) 整修房子

B 圈選出與中文意思相符的單字。

1　（某人）正在拖吊停車場裡的一輛卡車。

　➡ A truck in the parking lot is being (towed / loaded).

2　辦公室裡的每個人都正在審閱文件。

　➡ Everyone in the office is (putting on / reviewing) papers.

3　沿著火車鐵軌種下高大的樹木。

　➡ Tall trees are (mowed / planted) along the train tracks.

4　箱子整齊地堆放在地板上。

　➡ Boxes are (stacked / examined) neatly on the floor.

5　商店外面陳列著很多帽子。

　➡ A lot of hats have been (stared / displayed) outside the shop.

C 將括號內的單字按正確的順序排列組合成句子。

1　The old lady ⎯⎯⎯⎯⎯⎯⎯⎯⎯⎯⎯⎯.
　(potted / is / plants / watering)
　老太太正在給盆栽澆水。

2　The man ⎯⎯⎯⎯⎯⎯⎯⎯⎯⎯ in the living room.
　(taking / is / a coat / off)
　男子正在客廳脫外套。

3　A woman ⎯⎯⎯⎯⎯⎯⎯⎯⎯⎯ in a department store.
　(on / trying / is / a necklace)
　一名女子正在百貨公司試戴一條項鍊。

4　Cars ⎯⎯⎯⎯⎯⎯⎯⎯⎯⎯ the street.
　(have / along / parked / been)
　汽車沿著街道停放。

5　The young boy ⎯⎯⎯⎯⎯⎯⎯⎯⎯⎯ on the shelf.
　(for / reaching / is / a cell phone)
　那個小男孩正伸手去拿架上的手機。

PART 2

應答問題
Questions & Responses

01 WH 問句（1）who, what

Who

STEP 1　題型演練

Ⓐ 聆聽問句，並選出適當的回答。🎧 025

Q Who is working on the budget proposal? (A) Yes, we paid for it. (B) The general manger. (C) There has been a delay.	**Q.** 誰正在處理預算案？ (A) 是的，我們付過錢了。 (B) 總經理。 (C) 延誤了。

答案 (B)

▶ 本題詢問「誰正在處理預算案」，(B) 回答職稱「總經理」（The general manager）最為適當。WH 問句不能使用 Yes 或 No 回答，因此答案不能選 (A)。

🖉 解題重點

● 疑問詞 who 可當主詞或受詞。
　當作主詞使用時，句型為「**Who ＋動詞 ...?**」；當作受詞使用時，句型為「**Who ＋動詞＋主詞 ...?**」。
　Who is responsible for the presentation?〔**主詞＝「誰」**〕誰負責簡報？
　Who did you recommend for the project manager?〔**受詞＝「推薦誰」**〕
　你推薦誰當專案經理？
● 除了回答人名之外，還可以回答職位、職稱、部門名稱。
　職位、職稱：board of directors（董事會）、manager（經理）、representative（代表）、
　　　　　　　supervisor（主管）等
　部門名稱：R&D Department（研發部）、Sales Department（業務部）、Accounting
　　　　　　　Department（會計部）等

Ⓑ 聽完問句和答句後，選出相對應的回答。🎧 026

1　Who is the new sales manager?	(A) Sarah Baker. (B) I don't see it.
2　Who did you hire to renovate the office?	(A) The dealership. (B) Beetle Construction.
3　Who is in charge of the budget meeting?	(A) In the afternoon. (B) The sales supervisor.
4　Who should I talk to about the staff training?	(A) The Personnel Department. (B) It is next week.
5　Who has the budget proposal?	(A) I think Sarah has it. (B) In the cabinet.

字彙　**renovate** 整修　**budget** 預算　**staff training** 員工訓練　**proposal** 提案、計畫書

STEP 2 常考用法

請聆聽下列單字及片語，並跟著唸唸看。 🎧 027

Accounting Department	會計部	operating manager	營運經理
annual conference	年會	organizer	組織者、籌辦者
competitor	競爭對手	personal	個人的、親自的
evaluation	估價、評估	Sales Department	業務部
give a speech	發表演說	session	（從事某項活動的）一段時間
head	領導人、負責人	supervisor	主管
in person	親自、本人	work on	從事、處理

STEP 3 聽寫練習

先聆聽問句和答句，完成句子填空。接著再選出所有適當的回答。 🎧 028

1 Who ＿＿＿＿＿ the Peterson project?

(A) The projector is ＿＿＿＿＿.

(B) ＿＿＿＿＿ the ＿＿＿＿＿.

(C) Tim in the ＿＿＿＿＿.

2 Who should I ＿＿＿＿＿ about the ＿＿＿＿＿?

(A) The ＿＿＿＿＿.

(B) Ms. Kim ＿＿＿＿＿.

(C) Yes, you can ＿＿＿＿＿.

3 Who is ＿＿＿＿＿ the ＿＿＿＿＿?

(A) It's Ms. Rylan.

(B) No, ＿＿＿＿＿ it.

(C) ＿＿＿＿＿ have been finished.

4 ＿＿＿＿＿ at the annual conference?

(A) I am ＿＿＿＿＿.

(B) Employees ＿＿＿＿＿.

(C) He is ＿＿＿＿＿.

5 ＿＿＿＿＿ is going to ＿＿＿＿＿ at the seminar?

(A) ＿＿＿＿＿ Ann is.

(B) He was such an ＿＿＿＿＿.

(C) It ＿＿＿＿＿ yet.

6 ＿＿＿＿＿ is writing the ＿＿＿＿＿?

(A) ＿＿＿＿＿ it tomorrow.

(B) On the second floor.

(C) I'll ＿＿＿＿＿ and ＿＿＿＿＿.

What

A 聆聽問句,並選出適當的回答。 🎧 029

Q What time are we meeting with the new supplier? (A) Right after lunch. (B) The general manager. (C) A month ago.	**Q.** 我們什麼時候要和新的供應商碰面? (A) 就在午餐之後。 (B) 總經理。 (C) 一個月之前。 答案 (A)

▶ 請務必聽清楚 WH 問句的開頭部分「What time」(幾點)。本題詢問「什麼時候要和新的供應商碰面」,(A) 回答「就在午餐之後」(Right after lunch),告知特定的時間點,故為正確答案。

📝 解題重點

- 疑問詞 what 可當主詞或受詞。
  What happened in the meeting?〔主詞＝「什麼」事〕開會時發生了什麼事?
  What did you bring here?〔受詞＝「什麼」東西〕你帶了什麼來?
- 問句「**What do you think of . . . ?**」詢問的是對方的意見,意思為「你覺得……如何?」。
  What do you think of the new sales manager? 你覺得新的業務經理如何?
- 聽到以「**What ＋名詞**」開頭的 **WH** 問句時,請務必聽清楚疑問詞和名詞。
  What project are you working on? 你正在做什麼專案?

B 聽完問句和答句後,選出相對應的回答。 🎧 030

1 What did the Marketing Department ask for?	(A) Last year's sales records. (B) They had a lot of questions.
2 What is the best way to contact Mr. Han?	(A) You can share his contact details with me. (B) Probably his cell phone.
3 What do you think of the survey results?	(A) They should leave now. (B) They were satisfying.
4 What time can I check in to the hotel?	(A) Any time after three. (B) It should be cleaned.
5 What is the name of our new architect?	(A) Carol Smith, I think. (B) It's a good firm.

> 字彙 **ask for** 要求　**survey results** 調查結果　**contact details** 詳細聯絡方式　**satisfying** 令人滿意的　**any time** 隨時

STEP 2 常考用法

請聆聽下面單字，並跟著唸唸看。 🎧 031

accountant	會計師	membership fee	會員費
architect	建築師	recommend	推薦、建議
building directory	大樓住戶一覽表	sales representative	業務代表
creative	創造的、有創造力的	somewhere	在某處
crowded	擁擠的	tax form	報稅表格
floor plan	樓層平面圖	terrific	極好的

STEP 3 聽寫練習

先聆聽問句和答句，完成句子填空。接著再選出所有適當的回答。 🎧 032

1 What is the _____ at the yoga center?

　(A) All the _____ .

　(B) Thirty dollars _____ .

　(C) I am _____ .

2 What _____ the floor plan?

　(A) It's a _____ .

　(B) He is an _____ .

　(C) It needs to _____ .

3 _____ would you recommend?

　(A) Somewhere _____ .

　(B) I _____ it very _____ .

　(C) _____ this one here?

4 _____ is KT Technology on?

　(A) I am _____ it.

　(B) There's a _____ there.

　(C) They _____ it yet.

5 What did the _____ ?

　(A) No, the _____ did.

　(B) He just asked _____ .

　(C) The _____ .

6 _____ are you meeting with the lawyer?

　(A) Right _____ .

　(B) At 11 o'clock.

　(C) It's about the _____ .

實戰演練 Practice Test

A 聆聽問句和選項，並選出最適當的回答。 🎧033

1 Mark your answer on your answer sheet.　　(A)　(B)　(C)

2 Mark your answer on your answer sheet.　　(A)　(B)　(C)

3 Mark your answer on your answer sheet.　　(A)　(B)　(C)

4 Mark your answer on your answer sheet.　　(A)　(B)　(C)

5 Mark your answer on your answer sheet.　　(A)　(B)　(C)

6 Mark your answer on your answer sheet.　　(A)　(B)　(C)

7 Mark your answer on your answer sheet.　　(A)　(B)　(C)

8 Mark your answer on your answer sheet.　　(A)　(B)　(C)

9 Mark your answer on your answer sheet.　　(A)　(B)　(C)

10 Mark your answer on your answer sheet.　　(A)　(B)　(C)

B 再聽一遍問句和選項，並完成下面的句子填空。 034

1 _____ manager?

(A) This report is _____.

(B) He is _____.

(C) _____ from _____.

2 _____ does your train come?

(A) At Central Station.

(B) _____.

(C) _____ are quicker.

3 _____ the catering service
for the _____?

(A) I _____.

(B) Tom _____.

(C) The food was excellent.

4 _____
about the company's move?

(A) The _____.

(B) I _____ before.

(C) No, _____.

5 What kind of desk should we order for
our new office?

(A) I will _____.

(B) We need more chairs.

(C) No, _____.

6 _____ so long to finish
the _____?

(A) It is _____ this year.

(B) Alan helped me.

(C) I had a meeting to attend.

7 Who is in charge of _____
_____?

(A) I believe Emily is.

(B) It was _____.

(C) It's _____ from here.

8 _____ the
parade yesterday?

(A) Are you _____?

(B) Yes, it's on Sunday.

(C) It was _____.

9 _____ the applications?

(A) That sounds _____.

(B) About 5 million dollars.

(C) _____ did.

10 _____
the new _____?

(A) I _____.

(B) Ms. Cooper did.

(C) Yes, I work _____.

02 WH 問句（2）which, when

Which

STEP 1 題型演練

A 聆聽問句，並選出適當的回答。 `035`

Q Which of the proposals do you prefer?
(A) The one from Poly Technology.
(B) I have a good idea.
(C) I got a complaint.

Q. 你比較喜歡哪一個提案？
(A) 波利科技的那一個。
(B) 我有個好主意。
(C) 我接到投訴。

答案 (A)

▶ which 問句詢問的是對方的選擇。本題詢問對方「比較喜歡哪一個提案」，(A) 明確表示為「波利科技」這家公司的提案，故為正確答案。

解題重點

• 請熟記 which 問句的用法。which 問句的句型結構為「**which ＋名詞**」或「**which of the 複數名詞**」。
  Which bus should I take to go to the theater? 我該搭哪一班公車去劇院？
  Which of the applicants will you choose? 你會選哪一位應徵者？

• which 問句的回答方式可以明確表示選擇其中一項，也可以使用 **both**（兩者皆是）、**either**（兩者當中之一）、**neither**（兩者皆非）來回答。
  Q **Which of the applicants** will you choose? 你會選哪一位應徵者？
  A I like **neither**. 兩個我都不喜歡。 / I like **both**. 兩個我都喜歡。

B 聽完問句和答句後，選出相對應的回答。 `036`

1 Which class are you taking?	(A) The one about health care.
	(B) They don't offer it.
2 Which newspaper are you subscribing to?	(A) I don't enjoy reading.
	(B) The one you suggested yesterday.
3 Which of the departments is he going to?	(A) I don't think so.
	(B) Sales, I suppose.
4 Which one do you want to buy, the big one or the small one?	(A) I am afraid so.
	(B) Either is fine.
5 Which street is the bank on?	(A) You had better ask Carol.
	(B) I don't need to withdraw any money.

字彙 **health care** 醫療保健、健康照護　**subscribe to** 訂閱、訂購　**had better** 最好（做）……
withdraw 領（錢）

STEP 2 常考用法

請聆聽下列單字及片語，並跟著唸唸看。 🎧 037

be in charge of	負責……	process	處理
be interested in	對……感興趣	qualified	有資格的、勝任的
belong to	屬於……	reserve	預約、預訂
candidate	候選人、應徵者	tag	標籤
loan	借出、貸款	turn out	結果是……（尤指出乎意料的結果）

STEP 3 聽寫練習

先聆聽問句和答句，完成句子填空。接著再選出所有適當的回答。 🎧 038

1 _____ bag _____ to Mr. Evans?

(A) I _____ here.

(B) _____ the red tag.

(C) _____ in the _____ .

2 _____ of the I _____ ?

(A) _____ . I can _____ .

(B) The bookstore is _____ _____ .

(C) _____ is fine.

3 _____ of the _____ is _____ ?

(A) It is _____ .

(B) The team _____ .

(C) Ms. Rolling's _____ , _____ .

4 _____ of you is _____ ?

(A) Jeremy _____ .

(B) It was _____ .

(C) It _____ so well.

5 _____ do you want me to _____ a table at?

(A) The restaurant is _____ .

(B) _____ on Denver Street.

(C) I forgot to _____ .

6 _____ do you think is _____ ?

(A) The guy _____ .

(B) I don't _____ any _____ .

(C) It's been _____ .

STEP 1 題型演練

A 聆聽問句，並選出適當的回答。 🎧039

Q When do you expect the manager to arrive?	**Q.** 你預期經理何時會抵達？
(A) I expect so.	(A) 我預期如此。
(B) Next Wednesday, I suppose.	(B) 我想是下週三。
(C) I need your opinion.	(C) 我需要你的意見。
	答案 (B)

▶ when 問句詢問特定時間或時間點。本題詢問「預期經理何時會抵達」，(B) 明確表示時間為「下週三」，故為正確答案。

🅘 解題重點

- when 問句可以搭配過去式、現在式、未來式一起使用，因此答題重點在於選出與問句時態相符的答句。
  Q When do you think he **will arrive**?〔題目使用未來式〕你認為他何時會抵達？
  （×）**A** Last Friday. 上週五。※ 不能使用表示過去的副詞
  （○）**A** Next week. 下週。※ 答案為表示未來的副詞
- 雖然 when 問句詢問的是時間，但有時得選擇與時間無關的回答作為答案。
  Q When does the next train depart? 下一班火車何時發車？
  （○）**A** I am not sure. 我不確定。
  （○）**A** I'd better check the schedule. 我最好查一下時刻表。

B 聽完問句和答句後，選出所有相對應的回答。 🎧040

1	**When did** you **move** to this building?	(A) The previous one. (B) About 6 months ago.
2	**When are** you **planning to leave** this company?	(A) I need to talk to my supervisor first. (B) I don't live far from here.
3	**When should** we **discuss** the details of the contract?	(A) It's not that easy. (B) When will be good for you?
4	**When will** the package **be delivered**?	(A) I haven't ordered one. (B) Sometime next week.
5	**When do** we **have to finish** writing the report?	(A) No later than next Monday. (B) We at least need to do it.

> 字彙 **previous** 先前的　**supervisor** 主管　**deliver** 運送、投遞　**no later than** 不晚於……
> **at least** 至少

STEP 2 常考用法

請聆聽下列單字及片語，並跟著唸唸看。 🎧041

be supposed to	（被認為）應該……	postpone	延後、延期
business trip	出差、商務旅行	remind	提醒
by the end of the month	在月底之前	renovation	整修
company banquet	公司宴會	terrific	極好的
innovation	創新	work around the clock	日以繼夜地工作

STEP 3 聽寫練習

先聆聽問句和答句，完成句子填空。接著再選出所有適當的回答。 🎧042

1 _____ do we have to _____
our next _____ ?

(A) We'd _____ with the
manager.

(B) Last year's _____ was _____ .

(C) We _____ yet.

2 _____
from your business trip?

(A) _____ .

(B) Yesterday.

(C) I am _____ it.

3 _____ will _____ be
_____ ?

(A) It's _____ .

(B) By _____ .

(C) The _____ was successful.

4 _____ is _____ for
the project?

(A) It _____ until next
month.

(B) I am not _____ .

(C) I am _____ .

5 _____ we _____
meet our clients?

(A) The meeting was good.

(B) _____
yet.

(C) The _____ .

6 _____ should I _____ you
to leave?

(A) 30 minutes from now.

(B) This is a _____ .

(C) _____ .

實戰演練 Practice Test

Ⓐ 聆聽問句和選項，並選出最適當的回答。🎧 043

1 Mark your answer on your answer sheet.　　　(A)　　(B)　　(C)

2 Mark your answer on your answer sheet.　　　(A)　　(B)　　(C)

3 Mark your answer on your answer sheet.　　　(A)　　(B)　　(C)

4 Mark your answer on your answer sheet.　　　(A)　　(B)　　(C)

5 Mark your answer on your answer sheet.　　　(A)　　(B)　　(C)

6 Mark your answer on your answer sheet.　　　(A)　　(B)　　(C)

7 Mark your answer on your answer sheet.　　　(A)　　(B)　　(C)

8 Mark your answer on your answer sheet.　　　(A)　　(B)　　(C)

9 Mark your answer on your answer sheet.　　　(A)　　(B)　　(C)

10 Mark your answer on your answer sheet.　　　(A)　　(B)　　(C)

B 再聽一遍問句和選項，並完成下面的句子填空。🎧 044

PART

2

02 WH 問句（2）which, when

1 _____ do you want me to purchase?

(A) _____, the better.

(B) _____ one.

(C) It will cost a lot of money.

2 _____ will the consultants _____ in Seoul?

(A) At the end of the week.

(B) They will _____.

(C) Seoul is an _____.

3 _____ to get to the city?

(A) I _____ this area.

(B) Take the subway.

(C) The _____.

4 Which of these shirts _____ _____?

(A) Men's clothing.

(B) The _____.

(C) He _____ today.

5 Which day _____, Monday or Friday?

(A) I enjoyed _____.

(B) Today is Monday.

(C) _____ is better for me.

6 When is the quarterly report _____ _____?

(A) We are _____ now.

(B) We _____ last quarter.

(C) It _____.

7 _____ for the sales conference?

(A) It seems like _____.

(B) After work today.

(C) The _____ will be there.

8 Which of these products _____ _____?

(A) I got it.

(B) They _____ anymore.

(C) _____.

9 _____ are you working in, Accounting or Finance?

(A) I _____.

(B) _____ will be here.

(C) I haven't been there.

10 When do you think _____ _____?

(A) It's _____.

(B) It _____ already.

(C) Last Friday.

03 WH 問句（3）why, how

Why

Ⓐ 聆聽問句，並選出適當的回答。🎧 045

Q Why did the flight from London arrive so late?	Q. 從倫敦出發的班機為什麼這麼晚才抵達？
(A) Yes, it's a direct flight.	(A) 是的，是直飛的航班。
(B) I have been there recently.	(B) 我最近去過那裡。
(C) It was due to the bad weather.	(C) 因為天氣很糟的關係。
	答案 (C)

▶ 本題為 why 開頭的問句，詢問飛機延遲抵達的原因。(C) 使用片語「due to」（因為），直接解釋原因為「天氣很糟」（bad weather），故為正確答案。

🔖 解題重點

- 疑問詞 **why** 用來詢問原因或目的。
  若聽到選項中出現上面題目的「**due to**」，或是「**because** ＋子句 / **because of** ＋名詞」（因為）、「**to** ＋原形動詞」（為了……），有很高的機率是正確答案。

Q **Why** was Mr. Cole late for work today?	A **Because** he missed his bus.
科爾先生今天上班為什麼遲到？	因為他錯過了公車。
Q **Why** are you going to the warehouse?	A **To check** the inventory.
你為什麼要去倉庫？	為了去盤點庫存。

- 下列三種句型是以詢問的方式提出建議。
  ➡ **Why don't you . . . ?**（你何不……？）
  ➡ **Why don't we . . . ?**（我們何不……？／我們……吧？）
  ➡ **Why don't I . . . ?**（我……吧？）
  Why don't you go and help Helen? 你何不去幫海倫？
  Why don't I give you a ride to the airport? 我載你去機場吧？

Ⓑ 聽完問句和答句後，選出相對應的回答。🎧 046

1 **Why do you want** to get a refund?	(A) This product is damaged. (B) It's a five-percent discount.
2 **Why did you call** the warehouse manager?	(A) We have plenty. (B) To ask about the inventory.
3 **Why don't we look at** the survey results now?	(A) Sure. I have time. (B) Yes, that's good.
4 **Why is** Highway 82 **blocked**?	(A) We can go by car. (B) Because it's under construction.
5 **Why did** Samuel **leave** work today?	(A) On the second floor. (B) He has a medical checkup.

字彙 **refund** 退款、退還　**damaged** 受損的　**warehouse** 倉庫　**inventory** 存貨、存貨清單　**plenty** 充足、大量　**medical checkup** 健康檢查

STEP 2　常考用法

請聆聽下列單字及片語，並跟著唸唸看。 047

available	（人）有空的、（物）可用的、（物）可得到的	put off	延後、拖延
ceiling	天花板	recover	恢復、復原
consider	考慮	reschedule	重新安排……的時間
contest	競賽	sign up for	報名參加、註冊、申請
figure	數字、金額	water leak	漏水

STEP 3　聽寫練習

先聆聽問句和答句，完成句子填空。接著再選出所有適當的回答。 048

1 ＿＿＿＿＿＿ your furniture ＿＿＿＿＿＿ plastic?

(A) There's a ＿＿＿＿＿＿ in the ceiling.

(B) He will ＿＿＿＿＿＿ soon.

(C) ＿＿＿＿＿＿ to a new house.

2 ＿＿＿＿＿＿ we ＿＿＿＿＿＿ the sales meeting?

(A) It's on the third floor.

(B) Okay. Let's ＿＿＿＿＿＿.

(C) ＿＿＿＿＿＿ this Friday then?

3 ＿＿＿＿＿＿ the Accounting Department ＿＿＿＿＿＿?

(A) I ＿＿＿＿＿＿ yet.

(B) ＿＿＿＿＿＿ they did.

(C) The ＿＿＿＿＿＿ are wrong.

4 ＿＿＿＿＿＿ the international conference?

(A) Let me ＿＿＿＿＿＿.

(B) By airplane.

(C) Room 201 ＿＿＿＿＿＿.

5 Why don't you ＿＿＿＿＿＿ the contest?

(A) I'm ＿＿＿＿＿＿.

(B) That's a good idea.

(C) Because of the soccer game.

6 ＿＿＿＿＿＿ a laptop for the meeting?

(A) I ＿＿＿＿＿＿ one.

(B) I ＿＿＿＿＿＿ that.

(C) I think ＿＿＿＿＿＿ our new website.

How

A 聆聽問句，並選出適當的回答。 🎧049

Q How did the HR manager decide on the topic for the workshop? (A) The topic was too difficult. (B) He discussed it with the executives. (C) They are interviewing applicants.	**Q.** 人資經理是如何決定工作坊主題的？ (A) 那個主題太難了。 (B) 他和行政主管討論決定的。 (C) 他們正在面試應徵者。 答案 (B)

▶ 本題為疑問詞 how 開頭的問句，詢問「方法」。針對問題「如何決定工作坊主題」，(B) 表示「和行政主管討論」，指出具體的方法，故為正確答案。

📖 解題重點

- 疑問詞 **how** 用來詢問方法或手段。
  若選項出現「**by** ＋交通／聯絡方式」或「**by** ＋ **V-ing**」，便是正確答案。
  Q **How** did you contact Mr. Smith? 你是如何聯絡史密斯先生的？
  A **By email.** 用電子郵件。 / **By visiting** him in person. 我親自去拜訪的。
- 以「**How** ＋形容詞／副詞」開頭的問句，用來詢問數量、頻率或程度。
  How much did you pay for the printer? 你花多少錢買印表機的？
  How often do you go on a business trip? 你多久出一次差？
  How far is city hall from here? 市政府離這裡多遠？

B 聽完問句和答句後，選出相對應的回答。 🎧050

1 How should I submit the applications?	(A) It's Tuesday. (B) By mail.
2 How can I get to the airport?	(A) You can take the express train here. (B) By phone.
3 How often do you go to the fitness center?	(A) Twice a week. (B) By car.
4 How many chairs have been ordered?	(A) At the furniture shop. (B) A couple, I think.
5 How did you learn about the job opening?	(A) About a week ago. (B) I read about it in the newspaper.

字彙 **submit** 繳交、提出　**application** 申請表　**fitness center** 健身中心

STEP 2　常考用法

請聆聽下列單字及片語，並跟著唸唸看。 🎧 051

back up	備份	express mail	快捷郵件
competition	競爭、比賽	good deal	買得很便宜、很划算
detail	細節	hardly	幾乎不……
discount coupon	折價券	proposal	提案、計畫書
enter	進入	technician	技術人員

STEP 3　聽寫練習

先聆聽問句和答句，完成句子填空。接著再選出所有適當的回答。 🎧 052

1 _____ do you _____ your computer files?

(A) Very soon.

(B) Call a technician.

(C) I _____ it.

2 _____ to the post office from here?

(A) _____ a ten-minute walk.

(B) I _____.

(C) Twice a day.

3 _____ for IKM Technology?

(A) For about five years.

(B) Almost a year.

(C) By taxi.

4 _____ for the new construction project?

(A) I _____ by tomorrow.

(B) By _____.

(C) The road _____ now.

5 _____ the discount coupon?

(A) Yes, it's a good deal.

(B) Usually ten percent off.

(C) I printed it online.

6 _____ for the new laser printer?

(A) I don't remember exactly.

(B) From ten to twenty.

(C) The shop _____.

實戰演練 Practice Test

A 聆聽問句和選項，並選出最適當的回答。 053

1 Mark your answer on your answer sheet.　　　(A)　(B)　(C)

2 Mark your answer on your answer sheet.　　　(A)　(B)　(C)

3 Mark your answer on your answer sheet.　　　(A)　(B)　(C)

4 Mark your answer on your answer sheet.　　　(A)　(B)　(C)

5 Mark your answer on your answer sheet.　　　(A)　(B)　(C)

6 Mark your answer on your answer sheet.　　　(A)　(B)　(C)

7 Mark your answer on your answer sheet.　　　(A)　(B)　(C)

8 Mark your answer on your answer sheet.　　　(A)　(B)　(C)

9 Mark your answer on your answer sheet.　　　(A)　(B)　(C)

10 Mark your answer on your answer sheet.　　　(A)　(B)　(C)

B 再聽一遍問句和選項，並完成下面的句子填空。 🎧 054

1 _____ paper
from a different supplier?

(A) The price was _____.

(B) Through a _____.

(C) By Wednesday.

2 _____
the performance review tomorrow?

(A) It has been _____.

(B) It was a great concert.

(C) Sure. Tomorrow _____.

3 _____ to deliver
these clothes?

(A) Two to three days.

(B) Yes, it's _____.

(C) Shipping and handling _____
_____.

4 _____ is your company from
Central Station?

(A) It took me twenty minutes.

(B) It's _____ 100 meters.

(C) _____ a taxi?

5 _____ is the historic hotel on Pine
Street _____?

(A) Because it's _____.

(B) By tomorrow morning.

(C) I enjoyed _____.

6 _____ will you _____ with
the assignment?

(A) No, you said you would.

(B) _____ twenty minutes.

(C) Eric helped me a lot.

7 _____ take the afternoon
flight to Chicago?

(A) It won't _____.

(B) I _____ a morning flight.

(C) I leave at two o'clock.

8 Why did Mr. Tanaka _____
_____?

(A) I met him yesterday.

(B) By phone.

(C) Because sales are _____.

9 How do I _____?

(A) Please come in.

(B) The _____ a hundred dollars.

(C) You can _____ on our
website.

10 _____ the Gong Yoga
Center?

(A) I exercise every day.

(B) _____ down this
road.

(C) For ten minutes.

04 be 動詞開頭問句

現在式／過去式

STEP 1 題型演練

A 聆聽問句，並選出適當的回答。 🎧055

> **Q** Are you still available for Monday's meeting?
> (A) Yes, I will be there.
> (B) It will take a long time.
> (C) We should check on the availability.

> **Q.** 你週一還有空來參加會議嗎？
> (A) 是的，我會去。
> (B) 會花很長的時間。
> (C) 我們應該查看有空的時間。
>
> 答案 (A)

▶ 當題目為 be 動詞開頭的問句時，答案經常會使用 Yes/No 來回答。本題詢問「週一還有空來參加會議嗎」，(A) 表示會去，故為正確答案。

解題重點

- be 動詞開頭的問句分成現在式「**Is/Are/Am ＋主詞 . . . ?**」和過去式「**Was/Were ＋主詞 . . . ?**」兩種句型。請務必聽清楚題目開頭的部分，掌握問句的時態，才能避免選錯答案。
  Q **Is everything** ready for the workshop? 工作坊的東西都準備好了嗎？
  Q **Were you** at the dinner party yesterday? 你有去昨天的晚宴嗎？
- 題目為 be 動詞開頭的問句時，可以使用 **Yes/No** 來回答。但是有些時候會使用其他的答覆方式，當中不一定會出現 **Yes/No**。
  Q Are you still coming to the retirement party? 你還會來參加退休歡送會嗎？
  A I am still thinking about it. 我還在考慮。

B 聽完問句和答句後，選出相對應的回答。 🎧056

1 Is the recruiting process **finished** already?
(A) They will be chosen.
(B) It's not done yet.

2 Are you **looking for** something?
(A) No, I am just looking around.
(B) Yes, I will.

3 Are we **going to** review the proposal?
(A) When you have some time.
(B) No, it isn't.

4 Were you **able to** find a place to stay?
(A) Yes, we managed to get one.
(B) They were so helpful.

5 Is Ms. Takahashi **coming** to the reception tomorrow?
(A) She was there.
(B) I am not sure about it.

字彙 **recruiting** 招募、招聘　**look around** 四處看看、參觀　**review** 審閱　**proposal** 提案
manage to 設法做到……

STEP 2　常考用法

請聆聽下列單字及片語，並跟著唸唸看。 057

be opposed to	反對	keep -ing	持續做……
board meeting	董事會	presentation	簡報、演講
consultant	顧問	replacement	代替者、代替物
contact	聯絡	show up	露面、出席
financial	財務的、金融的	training course	訓練課程
get started	開始、著手	turn in one's resignation	（某人）遞出辭呈

STEP 3　聽寫練習

先聆聽問句和答句，完成句子填空。接著再選出所有適當的回答。 058

1 Was the _____ ?

(A) Yes, _____ financial problems.

(B) The _____ was about

_____ .

(C) I will _____ it.

2 Is the _____ for the
board meeting?

(A) They will _____ .

(B) I am still _____ it.

(C) Yes, it is _____ .

3 _____ join me for
dinner tonight?

(A) I already _____ .

(B) I am sorry. _____ .

(C) Yes, I _____ .

4 Is it Mr. Williams who _____ his
_____ ?

(A) That is _____ .

(B) They will _____ .

(C) No, it was Mr. Peterson.

5 _____ you _____ the
consultant?

(A) Yes, _____
soon.

(B) No, I am _____ .

(C) People will _____ .

6 _____ the director _____ be
at the meeting?

(A) I _____ for a few days.

(B) I suppose so.

(C) _____ be good.

be ＋ there ／未來式

A 聆聽問句，並選出適當的回答。🎧 059

Q Is there a cafeteria in this building?	**Q.** 這棟大樓裡有自助餐廳嗎？
(A) There is one on the third floor.	(A) 三樓有一間。
(B) Actually, I am not hungry.	(B) 我其實不餓。
(C) There is a nice café downtown.	(C) 市中心有一間很好的咖啡廳。

答案 (A)

▶ 題目開頭使用「Is there」，屬於 be 動詞開頭的問句。本題詢問「大樓裡有自助餐廳嗎」，(A) 回答「三樓有一間」，為適當的答覆。

📖 解題重點

- 問句使用「Is/Are there . . .」開頭時，詢問的是「有沒有……？」。
  Q **Is there** a gym in the basement? 地下室有健身房嗎？
  Q **Are there** laundry facilities in this building? 這棟大樓裡有洗衣設施嗎？
- be 動詞開頭的問句中，未來式的句型為「**Is/Are/Am ＋主詞＋ going to ＋原形動詞？**」或「**Will ＋主詞＋ be 動詞？**」。
  Q **Are** you **going to attend** the job fair? 你要參加公開徵才活動嗎？
  Q **Will** you **be** at tomorrow's lunch meeting? 你會參加明天的午餐會報嗎？

B 聽完問句和答句後，選出相對應的回答。🎧 060

1 **Are there any complaints** about the product?	(A) Not that I am aware of. (B) It was not produced.
2 **Are you going to leave** the company?	(A) I am seriously considering it. (B) I will apply for it.
3 **Is this going to be** his last chance?	(A) It is going to be easy. (B) I think so.
4 **Is there anything** planned for Jack's retirement?	(A) He will retire soon. (B) I don't know about that.
5 **Are there many people** at the gathering?	(A) Much more than I expected. (B) I just came back.

字彙 **not that I am aware of** 就我所知沒有、我不知道　**seriously** 認真地、嚴肅地　**consider** 考慮　**retirement** 退休

STEP 2 常考用法

請聆聽下列單字及片語，並跟著唸唸看。 061

additional	額外的	promotional event	促銷活動、宣傳活動
company banquet	公司宴會	Publicity Department	公關部
decision	決定	stationery store	文具店
fix	修理	supplies	用品
gathering	聚會、集會	upgrade	升級

STEP 3 聽寫練習

先聆聽問句和答句，完成句子填空。接著再選出所有適當的回答。 062

1 Are we _____
   _____?

   (A) The _____ is right over there.

   (B) _____.

   (C) I _____.

2 Is _____ this afternoon?

   (A) It _____.

   (B) _____ about it.

   (C) _____ it _____.

3 Are there any _____
   _____?

   (A) I _____.

   (B) In the _____.

   (C) I am _____.

4 _____ the _____
   to the company banquet tonight?

   (A) Sales _____.

   (B) I wasn't _____ it.

   (C) Yes, it's the _____.

5 Will you _____
   tomorrow's gathering?

   (A) Sorry. I have something else to do.

   (B) Nothing is available.

   (C) We have gathered _____
   _____.

6 Is Mike going to take the _____
   _____?

   (A) No, it's his day off.

   (B) Yes, he said he is going to _____
   _____.

   (C) We are _____.

A 聆聽問句和選項，並選出最適當的回答。 063

1　Mark your answer on your answer sheet.　　(A)　(B)　(C)

2　Mark your answer on your answer sheet.　　(A)　(B)　(C)

3　Mark your answer on your answer sheet.　　(A)　(B)　(C)

4　Mark your answer on your answer sheet.　　(A)　(B)　(C)

5　Mark your answer on your answer sheet.　　(A)　(B)　(C)

6　Mark your answer on your answer sheet.　　(A)　(B)　(C)

7　Mark your answer on your answer sheet.　　(A)　(B)　(C)

8　Mark your answer on your answer sheet.　　(A)　(B)　(C)

9　Mark your answer on your answer sheet.　　(A)　(B)　(C)

10　Mark your answer on your answer sheet.　　(A)　(B)　(C)

B 再聽一遍問句和選項，並完成下面的句子填空。🎧 064

1 _____ when you
were _____?
(A) Unfortunately, it _____.
(B) I had a _____.
(C) Yes, it was _____.

2 _____ the _____
come to Seoul?
(A) Yes, they said _____.
(B) He will _____.
(C) _____.

3 Was your _____?
(A) I am _____.
(B) _____ than I had expected.
(C) It _____.

4 Is _____ 24
hours a day?
(A) I _____ to _____ them.
(B) He _____.
(C) Yes, you can _____.

5 _____ you _____ to _____
_____?
(A) It's so _____.
(B) I am _____.
(C) Yes, I just _____.

6 Is there an _____?
(A) It's _____ to _____.
(B) It's _____.
(C) _____ no one.

7 Is she the one who is _____
_____?
(A) She is not a _____.
(B) I _____.
(C) _____ about it.

8 Is it _____ to _____
_____ this week?
(A) Of course. _____ will be
good for you?
(B) Sorry. I _____ it.
(C) I was _____.

9 _____ be free for next week's
dinner?
(A) No, I was busy.
(B) I need more time.
(C) I _____ for
2 weeks.

10 Were there _____
after the presentation?
(A) I _____ at it.
(B) There _____.
(C) Yes, that's _____ it _____
_____.

05 助動詞開頭問句

Do / Have

STEP 1 題型演練

Ⓐ 聆聽問句，並選出適當的回答。 🎧065

Q Do you want a drink while you are waiting?
(A) Yes, that would be great.
(B) We can reschedule it.
(C) You have to wait a long time.

Q. 你要不要邊等邊喝個東西？
(A) 好的，如果可以就太好了。
(B) 我們可以重新安排時間。
(C) 你得要等很久。

答案 (A)

▶ 問句使用一般動詞的現在式，因此請務必聽清楚「Do you」後方的動詞，掌握該動詞的意思。本題詢問對方是否要喝東西，(A) 給予肯定答覆，故為正確答案。

解題重點

- 一般動詞的問句，會根據主詞來決定句子開頭要使用 do 還是 does。若問句為過去式，則無論主詞為何，開頭皆使用 did。
  Do you want to join our club?〔**Do ＋ you ＋原形動詞？**〕你想要加入我們的俱樂部嗎？
  Does Eric plan to visit the New York office?〔**Does ＋ she/he/第三人稱單數＋原形動詞？**〕
  艾瑞克打算造訪紐約辦公室嗎？
  Did you review these documents?〔**Did ＋ you/he/she ＋原形動詞？**〕
  你審閱過這些文件了嗎？

- 詢問事情完成與否或是經驗時，會使用現在完成式問句（**Have/Has ＋主詞＋ p.p.?**）。
  Have you been to the new branch office in London?〔經驗〕
  你去過位於倫敦的新分公司嗎？
  Have you finished making the presentation for tomorrow?〔完成〕
  你做完明天要用的簡報了嗎？

Ⓑ 聽完問句和答句後，選出相對應的回答。 🎧066

1	**Did you attend** the finance conference last year?	(A) In Rome, Italy. (B) Yes, I went there last October.
2	**Have you finished** installing the new software on your computer?	(A) Yes, I had time yesterday. (B) He is a good technician.
3	**Do you have** time to review this report with me?	(A) Not until 3 o'clock. (B) It is on my desk.
4	**Does the restaurant open** on Sundays?	(A) I need to ask. (B) Lunch is ready.
5	**Have you accepted** articles from freelance writers?	(A) A few applicants. (B) No, I haven't done that yet.

字彙 **attend** 出席、參加 **install** 安裝 **review** 審閱 **report** 報告 **accept** 接受、認可 **article** 文章 **freelance writer** 自由作家

STEP 2 常考用法

請聆聽下列單字及片語，並跟著唸唸看。 🎧 067

accountant	會計師	membership card	會員卡
apply for	應徵、申請	release	發行、上市
deliver	運送、投遞	room	（會議）室、空間
lock	鎖住	storage room	儲藏室
Maintenance Department	維修部	yet	尚未

STEP 3 聽寫練習

先聆聽問句和答句，完成句子填空。接著再選出所有適當的回答。 🎧 068

1 Did you _____ with your _____ ?

(A) No, but I will.

(B) _____ are low.

(C) Yes, this morning.

2 _____ for KH Technology before?

(A) _____ at 2 P.M.

(B) No, I like my job.

(C) Yes, _____ .

3 Do they _____ at 6 o'clock?

(A) There is a lot of room.

(B) _____ Tim in the _____ .

(C) Mostly _____ .

4 _____ the new cell phone model _____ ?

(A) Sorry. We don't have it yet.

(B) Yes, _____ on your right.

(C) I bought a new laptop.

5 Do you want to _____ our store's membership card?

(A) We can _____ .

(B) No, thanks.

(C) Yes, that would be great.

6 Has Mr. Shin _____ New York yet?

(A) Yes, a few hours ago.

(B) No, he is _____ .

(C) He'd be _____ .

Can / Could / May / Should

A 聆聽問句，並選出適當的回答。 🎧069

Q Can you make a list of the guests for the company banquet? (A) Thanks. That's very nice of you. (B) I am planning to do that tomorrow. (C) For about 200 people.	**Q.** 你可以做一份公司宴會的賓客名單嗎？ (A) 謝謝，你人真好。 (B) 我正打算明天做。 (C) 大約 200 人的。 <div align="right">答案 (B)</div>

▶ 「Can you」開頭的問句詢問的是「可行性」。本題詢問是否能做一份名單，(B) 表示「打算明天做」，故為正確答案。

📖 解題重點

- 助動詞 can / could / may / should 詢問的是可行性／允許／建議等。助動詞開頭的問句句型為「助動詞＋主詞＋原形動詞」。

〔可行性〕　**Q** **Could/Can** you attend the awards ceremony on Tuesday evening?
　　　　　　你能參加週二晚上的頒獎典禮嗎？
　　　　　A Sorry. I will be working late. 抱歉，我要工作到很晚。

〔允許〕　　**Q** **May** I use this photocopier? 我可以用這台影印機嗎？
　　　　　　A Yes, press the red button to start. 可以，按下紅色按鈕就能啟動。

〔建議〕　　**Q** **Should** I turn on the air conditioning? 我該打開空調嗎？
　　　　　　A No, I will just open the windows. 不用，我打開窗戶就好。

B 聽完問句和答句後，選出相對應的回答。 🎧070

1 **Could you give** me a ride to work next week?	(A) Yes, you can ride my motorcycle. (B) My car broke down yesterday.
2 **Should we move** to a quieter location?	(A) That's a good idea. (B) They moved to a new apartment.
3 **May I help** you with anything?	(A) Call a shop assistant. (B) Not at the moment.
4 **Can you show** me how to start the projector?	(A) I can in 5 minutes. (B) Yes. It's in Room 608.
5 **Can I make** an international call from my hotel room?	(A) You can pay here. (B) Yes. It is free.

字彙 give . . . a ride 載……一程　break down 故障　shop assistant 店員
international call 國際電話

STEP 2　常考用法

請聆聽下列單字及片語，並跟著唸唸看。 071

advertisement	廣告	lab (= laboratory)	實驗室
advertisement	廣告	lab (= laboratory)	實驗室
bargain	（划算的）交易	pleased	高興的、滿意的
ceremony	儀式、典禮	promotional event	促銷活動、宣傳活動
client	客戶	proposal	提案、計畫書
figure	數字、金額	review	審閱
first thing	一大早	wait until	等到……

STEP 3　聽寫練習

先聆聽問句和答句，完成句子填空。接著再選出所有適當的回答。 072

1 _____ to our client's office this afternoon?

(A) Our customers are very pleased.

(B) It is _____.

(C) I _____ my car.

2 May I _____ the lab test results?

(A) Where is the laboratory?

(B) _____.

(C) They are _____.

3 _____ the new sales figures this morning?

(A) We did _____.

(B) _____ until this afternoon.

(C) That's _____.

4 Should I _____ to develop our new product's design?

(A) I think that's a _____.

(B) I'm planning to buy it.

(C) The color is _____.

5 Could you _____ we created?

(A) _____ tomorrow morning.

(B) For twenty minutes.

(C) _____ this morning.

6 Can you _____ on Wednesday?

(A) Sure. What time is it?

(B) Well, I don't think _____.

(C) Congratulations.

實戰演練 Practice Test

A 聆聽問句和選項，並選出最適當的回答。 🎧 073

1 Mark your answer on your answer sheet.　　　(A)　(B)　(C)

2 Mark your answer on your answer sheet.　　　(A)　(B)　(C)

3 Mark your answer on your answer sheet.　　　(A)　(B)　(C)

4 Mark your answer on your answer sheet.　　　(A)　(B)　(C)

5 Mark your answer on your answer sheet.　　　(A)　(B)　(C)

6 Mark your answer on your answer sheet.　　　(A)　(B)　(C)

7 Mark your answer on your answer sheet.　　　(A)　(B)　(C)

8 Mark your answer on your answer sheet.　　　(A)　(B)　(C)

9 Mark your answer on your answer sheet.　　　(A)　(B)　(C)

10 Mark your answer on your answer sheet.　　　(A)　(B)　(C)

B 再聽一遍問句和選項，並完成下面的句子填空。 🎧 074

1 Could you _____
  this machine?

  (A) It is _____ .

  (B) _____ to this, too.

  (C) Suzanne called you earlier.

2 Should we _____ on
  the patio _____ ?

  (A) _____ cold?

  (B) I'll have coffee.

  (C) Three people _____ .

3 Did you _____ this
  afternoon?

  (A) Oh, no. I forgot.

  (B) Please _____ .

  (C) I have _____ .

4 _____ a little
  earlier today?

  (A) In fact, she was _____
      _____ .

  (B) It _____ .

  (C) Sure. Are you okay?

5 _____
  to the new French restaurant?

  (A) You need _____
      _____ .

  (B) _____ meet at 3:30?

  (C) Yes, it's the best place _____
      _____ .

6 _____
  for the opening game of the
  championship?

  (A) Yes, a month ago.

  (B) The show is on Sunday.

  (C) _____ .

7 Do you think _____
  _____ ?

  (A) It _____ .

  (B) No, it was created by Mark.

  (C) Just _____ .

8 _____ to Ms.
  Gray's farewell party?

  (A) She is _____ .

  (B) At the Hill Hotel.

  (C) I don't have _____ .

9 Can you make the speech no longer
  than twenty minutes?

  (A) Okay, I will _____ .

  (B) It was _____ .

  (C) The speech was _____ .

10 Does _____
  every year?

  (A) Every two years.

  (B) I like _____ .

  (C) It started yesterday.

A 選出正確的中文意思。

1 budget proposal　　　　　　(A) 預算審核　　　　(B) 預算案
2 annual conference　　　　　(A) 年會　　　　　　(B) 月會
3 operating manager　　　　　(A) 營運經理　　　　(B) 營運系統
4 company banquet　　　　　 (A) 公司宴會　　　　(B) 公司同事
5 promotional event　　　　　(A) 升遷活動　　　　(B) 促銷活動

B 圈選出與中文意思相符的單字。

1 你可以教我如何操作這台機器嗎？

➡ Could you show me how to (operate / manage) this machine?

2 我在哪裡可以找到大樓住戶一覽表？

➡ Where can I find a (building directory / building blueprint)?

3 你把他歡送會的邀請函寄出去了嗎？

➡ Have you sent out the invitations to his (retirement party / farewell party)?

4 您想要申辦我們店裡的會員卡嗎？

➡ Do you want to (sign up for / apply to) our store's membership card?

5 會計要求什麼東西？

➡ What did the accountant (apply for / ask for)?

C 將括號內的單字按正確的順序排列組合成句子。

1 It _____ yet. (not / decided / has / been)

還沒有決定。

2 _____ the new work shifts? (do / think / of / you / what)

你覺得新的班表如何？

3 Who is _____ the workshop? (of / organizing / charge / in)

誰負責籌備工作坊？

4 When _____ our clients? (meet / to / we / supposed / are)

我們應該何時和我們的客戶碰面？

5 _____ are made locally? (of / these / which / products)

這些產品裡有哪些是在本地製造的？

06 間接問句／選擇性疑問句

間接問句

STEP 1　題型演練

Ⓐ 聆聽問句，並選出適當的回答。🎧 075

Q Do you know where the Payroll Department is?

(A) I was not paid for it.

(B) About thirty minutes from now.

(C) Ask David.

> Q. 你知道薪資部在哪裡嗎？
>
> (A) 我沒有拿到錢。
>
> (B) 從現在起大約 30 分鐘後。
>
> (C) 問大衛。
>
> 答案 (C)

▶ 本題的句型結構為「Do you know ＋疑問詞＋主詞＋動詞」，屬於間接問句，詢問「薪資部在哪裡」。
(C) 提出解決方式為「問大衛」，故為正確答案。

🗒 解題重點

- 請記住間接問句的句型結構。

  Do you know <u>where</u> the cafeteria is?〔**Do you know** ＋疑問詞＋主詞＋動詞**？**〕
  你知道自助餐廳在哪裡嗎？

  Did you hear <u>who</u> is going to take over the job?〔**Did you hear** ＋疑問詞＋主詞＋動詞**？**〕
  你有聽說是誰要接這個工作嗎？

  Can you tell me <u>why</u> she refused the offer?〔**Can you tell me** ＋疑問詞＋主詞＋動詞**？**〕
  你可以告訴我為什麼她拒絕這個工作邀約嗎？

- 請務必聽清楚間接問句當中的疑問詞。

  Q Can you tell me **why** she quit her job? 你可以告訴我她為什麼辭職嗎？

  A **Because** she wasn't happy with the salary. 因為她對薪水不滿意。

Ⓑ 聽完問句和答句後，選出相對應的回答。🎧 076

1 Do you know when the next train is coming?	(A) In about 30 minutes. (B) It's not fixed yet.
2 Did you hear who is giving a speech?	(A) He is a good speaker. (B) Mr. Dobbins will.
3 Can you tell me where the meeting will be held?	(A) At the conference hall. (B) Sorry. I couldn't.
4 May I ask where you are working?	(A) I am currently unemployed. (B) I am working on the project.
5 Could you tell me what time the bank will open?	(A) It's closed now. (B) Usually at 9 in the morning.

字彙 **give a speech** 發表演說　**be held**（活動）舉行　**currently** 目前　**unemployed** 失業的、待業的

請聆聽下列單字及片語，並跟著唸唸看。 🎧077

awful	極糟的、可怕的	proposal	提案、計畫書
budget	預算	public transportation	大眾運輸
hire	僱用	quarter	季
how often	多常（做）……	R&D Department (= Research and Development Department)	研發部
issue	問題、爭議	sales figures	銷售數字、銷售額
lead	領導	what . . . like	（某人／某物）怎麼樣

STEP 3 聽寫練習

先聆聽問句和答句，完成句子填空。接著再選出所有適當的回答。 🎧078

1 Do you know why the ＿＿＿＿＿ is
＿＿＿＿＿＿＿＿＿＿＿＿＿？

   (A) We are still ＿＿＿＿＿.

   (B) It needs one ＿＿＿＿＿.

   (C) Because it isn't ＿＿＿＿＿.

2 Can you tell me ＿＿＿＿＿＿＿＿＿
the ＿＿＿＿＿＿＿？

   (A) ＿＿＿＿＿＿＿.

   (B) The traffic is ＿＿＿＿＿.

   (C) ＿＿＿＿＿＿＿＿＿＿ would
be nice.

3 Do you know ＿＿＿ the ＿＿＿＿＿
＿＿＿＿＿＿＿ this quarter?

   (A) The ＿＿＿＿＿＿＿.

   (B) I ＿＿＿＿＿ it.

   (C) I haven't ＿＿＿＿＿＿＿
them.

4 Did you hear ＿＿＿＿＿＿ to the
R&D Department?

   (A) I didn't ＿＿＿＿＿ her.

   (B) I ＿＿＿＿＿＿＿＿＿.

   (C) Mr. Cummings ＿＿＿＿＿.

5 Could you tell me ＿＿＿＿＿＿＿＿
like the ＿＿＿＿＿？

   (A) I ＿＿＿＿＿＿＿＿ it.

   (B) He ＿＿＿＿＿.

   (C) The ＿＿＿＿＿＿＿＿＿＿.

6 Do you ＿＿＿＿＿ where the
contracts are?

   (A) You've already answered it.

   (B) They are ＿＿＿＿＿＿＿.

   (C) Actually, I was ＿＿＿＿＿＿,
too.

60

選擇性疑問句

A 聆聽問句，並選出適當的回答。 🎧079

Q Do you want to leave now, or should I wait a few more minutes?
(A) I am ready to go.
(B) I should wait for you.
(C) I need more patience.

Q. 你想現在走，還是我要再等幾分鐘？
(A) 我準備好要走了。
(B) 我應該等你。
(C) 我得更有耐心一點。

答案 (A)

▶ 選擇性疑問句考的是從兩個選項中擇一。本題詢問「你想現在走，還是我要再等幾分鐘」。(A) 表示「我準備好要走了」，從中選擇一種行動，故為正確答案。

解題重點

- 選擇性疑問句會提供兩個選項，要求聽者從中作出選擇。題目句會使用連接詞 or（或者、還是）來連接名詞、片語或子句。
  Would you like **coffee or tea**?〔名詞＋名詞〕
  你要喝咖啡還是茶？
  Do you want to **go to the movies or relax at home**?〔動詞片語＋動詞片語〕
  你想去看電影，還是在家休息？
- 選擇性疑問句的答案可以是：兩種選擇都不要、兩種選擇都要，或提出第三種選擇。
  Q Will you sign up for the training session for today or tomorrow?
  你會報名參加今天的訓練課程，還是明天的？
  A Neither. 兩天都不報名。 / Both. 兩天都報名。 /
  I will do it next month. 我下個月再報名參加。

B 聽完問句和答句後，選出相對應的回答。 🎧080

1 Are you going to read **a paper or a magazine**?	(A) Neither. I want to relax. (B) I tried both of them.
2 Do you prefer working **in the morning or in the afternoon**?	(A) I am so tired. (B) I am a morning person.
3 Will you pay **in cash or by credit card**?	(A) It wasn't paid. (B) I don't have enough cash.
4 Would you like **beef or chicken**?	(A) Neither. I am not hungry. (B) I had both of them.
5 **Do you want me to help you, or can you do it alone**?	(A) I can take care of it myself. (B) I will join you.

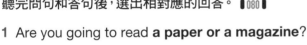

字彙 morning person 習慣早起的人　in cash 用現金（支付）　enough 足夠的　take care of 處理

請聆聽下列單字及片語，並跟著唸唸看。 🎧081

Accounting	會計部	go with	選擇、接受
business trip	出差	preference	偏好
Finance	財務部	qualified	有資格的、勝任的
flexible	有彈性的	The more, the better.	愈多愈好。
go on a business trip	去出差	would rather	寧願……、較喜歡……

先聆聽問句和答句，完成句子填空。接著再選出所有適當的回答。 🎧082

1 Would you like to .... or the blue one?

(A) I like neither.

(B) I don't ....

(C) I will .... the red one.

2 .... a business trip on .... or .... ?

(A) Neither. It ....

(B) I don't ....

(C) Let's ....

3 .... to work in .... or .... ?

(A) No, thanks.

(B) .... is ....

(C) I .... go there.

4 .... is .... for the job, Georgia or you?

(A) ...., ...

(B) .... are unhappy.

(C) It's ....

5 Would you .... or .... ?

(A) I'd ....

(B) My .... is ....

(C) I don't ....

6 Will you be able to ...., or .... more?

(A) I .... in a few minutes.

(B) I can do it ....

(C) I am not ....

實戰演練 Practice Test

A 聆聽問句和選項，並選出最適當的回答。 🎧 083

1 Mark your answer on your answer sheet.　　　　(A)　(B)　(C)

2 Mark your answer on your answer sheet.　　　　(A)　(B)　(C)

3 Mark your answer on your answer sheet.　　　　(A)　(B)　(C)

4 Mark your answer on your answer sheet.　　　　(A)　(B)　(C)

5 Mark your answer on your answer sheet.　　　　(A)　(B)　(C)

6 Mark your answer on your answer sheet.　　　　(A)　(B)　(C)

7 Mark your answer on your answer sheet.　　　　(A)　(B)　(C)

8 Mark your answer on your answer sheet.　　　　(A)　(B)　(C)

9 Mark your answer on your answer sheet.　　　　(A)　(B)　(C)

10 Mark your answer on your answer sheet.　　　　(A)　(B)　(C)

1 _____ mail this, or
_____ to the post office
yourself?
(A) Jack _____ this afternoon.
(B) I _____ it.
(C) The _____ will _____.

2 Can you _____ you _____
_____ the firm?
(A) I _____.
(B) There is _____.
(C) I _____ my _____.

3 _____ dinner _____
or sometime _____?
(A) I am _____.
(B) I _____.
(C) Dinner _____.

4 Did you _____ is going to
_____ the position?
(A) No one _____.
(B) Jack _____.
(C) The _____ are over
there.

5 Should I _____
today or next week?
(A) We can _____.
(B) The _____ is
closed.
(C) You _____.

6 Do you know _____ the _____
is _____?
(A) They will _____.
(B) We _____.
(C) _____ on that for you.

7 _____ what kind of job you had
_____?
(A) I _____ it before.
(B) I was _____.
(C) Please _____.

8 _____, or do you want
me to _____ a little longer?
(A) It's _____.
(B) I can't _____ here.
(C) _____ I know.

9 Do you know _____
_____ is?
(A) Just _____.
(B) _____, it is not on sale.
(C) I _____ this area.

10 Do you _____
the report, or _____ it
yourself?
(A) _____ it.
(B) _____.
(C) I _____.

07 附加問句／否定疑問句

附加問句

STEP 1　題型演練

Ⓐ 聆聽問句，並選出適當的回答。 🎧085

> **Q** You haven't called Maintenance about the copier, have you?
> (A) I need five copies.
> (B) No, they are coming to fix it.
> (C) Is it broken again?

> **Q.** 你還沒打電話給維修部請他們來看影印機，對吧？
> (A) 我需要五份。
> (B) 對，他們會來修。
> (C) 又故障了嗎？
> 答案 (C)

▶ 本題為「肯定形式」的附加問句。(C) 採反問方式答覆，故為正確答案。(B) 要將 No 改成 Yes，表示「不，剛剛已經打過電話，他們會過來修理」（注意此處的 Yes 須理解為「不」），才能作為答案。

📖 解題重點

- 欲向對方確認或取得同意時，會使用附加問句。肯定句後方要加上「否定附加問句」；否定句後方則要加上「肯定附加問句」。
  You **have seen** the report, **haven't you**? 〔肯定句＋否定附加問句〕你看過報告了，不是嗎？
  She **didn't** return my call, **did** she? 〔否定句＋肯定附加問句〕她沒有回我電話，對嗎？

- 回答附加問句時，表示肯定要用 Yes，表示否定則要用 No。
  只要轉換成肯定附加問句來理解，就不會搞不清楚要用 Yes 還是用 No 回答。
  Q You have eaten, haven't you? 你吃過了，不是嗎？
  A **Yes**, I have. / **No**, I haven't. 對，我吃過了。／不，我還沒吃。

  Q You haven't eaten, have you? 你還沒吃，對嗎？
  A **Yes**, I have. / **No**, I haven't. 不，我吃過了。／對，我還沒吃。
  ※ 請注意，上面的第二個對話中，Yes 須理解為「不」，No 須理解為「對」

Ⓑ 聽完問句和答句後，選出相對應的回答。 🎧086

1 You **haven't submitted** your assignment yet, **have you**?	(A) The interview went well. (B) No, probably after lunch.
2 You **are not working** late tonight, **are you**?	(A) No, I'm a bit tired. (B) Yes, I am ready to leave.
3 Mr. May **received** a pay raise, **didn't he**?	(A) Where did you hear that? (B) Yes, he moved to a sales team.
4 Jane **hasn't taken** inventory yet, **has she**?	(A) You can take two. (B) No, she looked busy.
5 I **should cancel** the meeting, **shouldn't I**?	(A) That would be better. (B) Wasn't it in room 3?

 字彙 **submit** 繳交、提出　**assignment** 工作　**pay raise** 加薪　**take inventory** 盤點存貨

65

請聆聽下列單字及片語，並跟著唸唸看。 🎧087

afraid	害怕的、恐怕、遺憾	have been to	曾去過……
dentist	牙醫	look into	調查、深入檢查
express mail	快捷郵件	projector	投影機
fix	修理	used to	過去經常……、過去習慣……

先聆聽問句和答句，完成句子填空。接著再選出所有適當的回答。 🎧088

1 _____ Spain, haven't you?

(A) Yes, three times.

(B) _____ I haven't.

(C) He just _____.

2 There is a post office around the corner, _____?

(A) _____.

(B) The shop is closed.

(C) _____ down the road.

3 You _____ Dr. Petal, _____?

(A) Yes, this morning.

(B) I need to see the dentist.

(C) _____?

4 You _____ your flight, have you?

(A) Actually, I just did.

(B) I _____.

(C) No, _____ lately.

5 The projector _____, _____?

(A) We might need a new one.

(B) I need to _____.

(C) I just _____.

6 Mr. Anderson _____, _____?

(A) Yes, _____ yesterday.

(B) I think _____.

(C) The documents _____ _____.

否定疑問句

STEP 1　題型演練

A 聆聽問句，並選出適當的回答。🎧 089

Q Doesn't Mr. Lawrence want to book a window seat?

(A) It is in Aisle 2.

(B) His flight has been delayed.

(C) Yes, he likes to look out the window.

Q. 羅倫斯先生不是想要預訂靠窗的座位嗎？

(A) 在第二排。

(B) 他的班機誤點了。

(C) 是的，他喜歡看窗外。

答案 (C)

▶ 本題使用否定詞 not，屬於否定疑問句，詢問「是否想要靠窗的座位」。(C) 回答完 Yes 後，解釋其原因，故為正確答案。

📖 解題重點

- 否定疑問句中包含否定詞 not，用於確認資訊或提供對方建議。

  Didn't anybody hear about the survey results? 沒有任何人聽說調查結果嗎？

  Haven't you joined the fitness center downtown? 你不是加入了城裡的健身中心嗎？

  Can't you attend the conference on Monday? 你不能參加週一的研討會嗎？

- 只要將否定疑問句轉換成肯定疑問句思考，就不會搞不清楚要用 Yes 還是用 No 回答。

  Q **Aren't** you going to come to the party? 你不來派對嗎？

  A 〔肯定答覆〕**Yes**, I'm coming.　　〔否定答覆〕**No**, I'm too busy.

  　　　　　　不，我會去。　　　　　　　　　對，我太忙了。

  ※ 請注意此處 Yes 須理解為「不」，No 須理解為「對」

B 聽完問句和答句後，選出相對應的回答。🎧 090

1 **Isn't there** a department store close by?

(A) The road is closed now.
(B) Yes, it's around the corner.

2 **Haven't** you **delivered** the package to Mr. Ford?

(A) Sorry. I will do it right away.
(B) Yes, it is downstairs.

3 **Didn't** your car **break down** last week?

(A) I already did that.
(B) Yes, it is still in the repair shop.

4 **Isn't** your doctor's appointment **this morning**?

(A) Thank you for reminding me.
(B) He is an excellent surgeon.

5 **Doesn't** Diane normally **arrive** here at three?

(A) Yes, but she is sick today.
(B) We are late for work.

字彙 department store 百貨公司　close by 在旁邊　around the corner 在附近　deliver 運送、投遞
package 包裹　break down 故障　appointment（會面的）約定　remind 提醒
surgeon 外科醫生

STEP 2　常考用法

請聆聽下列單字及片語，並跟著唸唸看。 🎧 091

be supposed to	（被認為）應該……	organize	組織、籌備、安排
call in sick	打電話請病假	reschedule	重新安排……的時間
not that I know of	就我所知並非如此	retirement	退休
on one's way	（某人）在去……的途中	sign up	報名參加、註冊
on vacation	在度假	work on	從事、處理

STEP 3　聽寫練習

先聆聽問句和答句，完成句子填空。接著再選出所有適當的回答。 🎧 092

1 .... Ms. Rice at work this morning?

(A) At three in the afternoon.

(B) She ....

(C) I think Kelly might know.

2 .... on vacation?

(A) Yes, but I ....

(B) I'm going to Hawaii.

(C) No, it is next week.

3 ....

after lunch?

(A) Sorry. I am busy all afternoon.

(B) I don't think so.

(C) ....

4 .... Ms. Hunt's retirement party?

(A) She is ....

(B) I ....

(C) She said she didn't want any.

5 .... coming today?

(A) No, they ....

(B) .... next Monday.

(C) Why .... ?

6 ....

attend the conference in London?

(A) No, it ....

(B) She isn't going.

(C) Mr. Lim .... it.

實戰演練 Practice Test

A 聆聽問句和選項，並選出最適當的回答。🎧093

1 Mark your answer on your answer sheet.　　　(A)　(B)　(C)

2 Mark your answer on your answer sheet.　　　(A)　(B)　(C)

3 Mark your answer on your answer sheet.　　　(A)　(B)　(C)

4 Mark your answer on your answer sheet.　　　(A)　(B)　(C)

5 Mark your answer on your answer sheet.　　　(A)　(B)　(C)

6 Mark your answer on your answer sheet.　　　(A)　(B)　(C)

7 Mark your answer on your answer sheet.　　　(A)　(B)　(C)

8 Mark your answer on your answer sheet.　　　(A)　(B)　(C)

9 Mark your answer on your answer sheet.　　　(A)　(B)　(C)

10 Mark your answer on your answer sheet.　　　(A)　(B)　(C)

1 _____
the office at five?

(A) She is my _____.

(B) No, we _____.

(C) Yes, but she _____
today.

2 These umbrellas _____
by our new supplier, _____?

(A) No, it _____.

(B) Maybe next month.

(C) No, _____.

3 Ms. Forster _____
_____, has she?

(A) She did yesterday.

(B) About _____.

(C) At the staff meeting.

4 You said the _____
this week, _____?

(A) No, he will _____.

(B) Yes, it is _____.

(C) Five days ago.

5 _____ to Mongolia
at the end of this month?

(A) I prefer an aisle seat.

(B) No, _____.

(C) _____ a travel agency.

6 Ms. Kelly will _____,
won't she?

(A) Yes, she said she'd do that.

(B) When did _____?

(C) Her office is _____.

7 Isn't there a job opening on the
accounting team?

(A) You are _____.

(B) The shop _____ right now.

(C) _____ are a little off.

8 You _____
we interviewed today, didn't you?

(A) He is _____ for
the job.

(B) The job interview _____.

(C) We will hire only _____.

9 _____
on June 17?

(A) I was deeply impressed with that.

(B) It _____.

(C) No, for twenty days.

10 You _____ the text size, _____
_____?

(A) Yes, it was too small.

(B) No, the room is big.

(C) The printer _____.

08 表示建議的問句／表示要求的問句

表示建議的問句

STEP 1 題型演練

A 聆聽問句，並選出適當的回答。 🎧095

Q Why don't we make a reservation first?

(A) I already did that.

(B) Because I was busy.

(C) Of course not.

> Q. 我們何不先訂位？
>
> (A) 我已經訂位了。
>
> (B) 因為我當時很忙。
>
> (C) 當然不是。
>
> 答案 (A)

▶ 本題的句型結構為「Why don't we ＋原形動詞」，表示建議，詢問「何不先訂位」。(A) 回答「已經訂位了」，故為正確答案。

🅾 解題重點

* 請記住下面的表示建議的句型。

Why don't you/we go for a walk?
（何不……？）你／我們何不去散個步？

How about sending him an invitation?
（……如何？）寄張邀請卡給他如何？

Would you like to take a look at the brochure?
（想要……嗎？）你想要看一下小冊子嗎？

Would you like me to take notes on it?
（要不要我……？）要不要我把它記下來？

* 請一併記住表示同意或拒絕的答覆方式。

〔表示同意〕	Okay. 好。 / Sure. 當然好。 / That's a good idea. 那是個好主意。 That sounds good. 聽起來不錯。 / That would be great. 如果可以就太好了。
〔表示拒絕〕	I am sorry, but . . . 抱歉，但是…… / I'd rather not. 我不想這樣做。 I already did. 我已經做了。 / Let me think about it. 讓我想一想。

B 聽完問句和答句後，選出相對應的回答。 🎧096

1 **How about** canceling the next board meeting?	(A) I don't think that's a good idea. (B) We arranged it.
2 **Why don't we** call a technician?	(A) That sounds good. (B) I didn't do it.
3 **Why don't you** print the results?	(A) It is due on Monday. (B) Sorry, but the printer is broken.
4 **Would you like me to** drop it off in your office?	(A) I'd rather not. (B) I would appreciate it.
5 **Would you like to** take a quick break?	(A) I'd rather not. (B) It broke down.

字彙 **board meeting** 董事會會議　**technician** 技術人員　**print** 印刷
drop . . . off 將……捎帶至（某地）　**appreciate** 感謝

請聆聽下列單字及片語，並跟著唸唸看。 🎧097

brochure	小冊子、資料手冊	sales representative	業務代表
deliver	運送、投遞	take a look at	看一看……
had better	最好（做）……	technician	技術人員
hear about	聽說……	training session	訓練課程
promote	提升、促進	You bet.	當然（好）。

STEP 3 聽寫練習

先聆聽問句和答句，完成句子填空。接著再選出所有適當的回答。 🎧098

1 _____ have _____ ?

(A) Great. I am hungry.

(B) I think _____ .

(C) Yes, I _____ it was _____ .

2 _____ a training session for the _____ ?

(A) _____ .

(B) I am sorry, but _____ .

(C) I didn't like it.

3 _____ some brochures?

(A) I already _____ .

(B) You'd better _____ .

(C) That _____ .

4 _____ move these cabinets _____ ?

(A) _____ .

(B) That's a good idea.

(C) _____ a technician.

5 _____ hire more sales representatives to _____ ?

(A) I'd love to, but we _____ _____ .

(B) Okay, I've _____ it.

(C) I _____ .

6 Would you like me to _____ while I am _____ ?

(A) That _____ .

(B) You _____ .

(C) _____ do it.

表示要求的問句

Ⓐ 聆聽問句，並選出適當的回答。🎧 099

Q Could you mail these documents to the London branch?

(A) Sure, I can do that.

(B) I will email you.

(C) They are hard to get.

Q. 你可以把這些文件寄去倫敦分公司嗎？

(A) 當然好，我可以去寄。

(B) 我會發電子郵件給你。

(C) 那些很難拿到。

答案 (A)

▶ 本題為「Could you . . .」開頭的問句，表示要求。(A) 表示接受將文件寄送至倫敦分公司的要求，故為正確答案。

🖒解題重點

● 請記住下面表示要求的句型。

Can I give you a call if I have a question?

（我可以……嗎？）如果我有問題，可以打電話給你嗎？

Will/Would you help me do this?（你可以……嗎？）你可以協助我做這件事嗎？

Can/Could you give me a ride to the airport?（你可以……嗎？）你可以載我去機場嗎？

Do/Would you mind leaving the door open?（你介意……嗎？）你介意讓門開著嗎？

● 請特別留意「**Do/Would you mind . . . ?**」的回答方式。mind 表示「介意、不喜歡」之意，因此回答 **No** 表示「同意」、回答 **Yes** 則是表示「拒絕」。

Q **Do you mind** leaving the door open? 你介意讓門開著嗎？

〔同意〕**A** | **Not** at all. 一點也不。

　　　　 | Of course **not**. 當然不會。

〔拒絕〕**A** Sorry, but **yes**. 抱歉，但我介意。

Ⓑ 聽完問句和答句後，選出相對應的回答。🎧 100

1 **Can I** get an information sheet about this area?	(A) Of course. Here you are. (B) We don't have any money in the budget.
2 **Will you** help me to move this table?	(A) I am fine. Thanks. (B) Sure, when do you want me to do it?
3 **Do you mind** turning down the volume?	(A) The music wasn't very good. (B) Sorry. I didn't know it was loud.
4 **Can you** drop this off at the office?	(A) No, I already finished it. (B) Yes, I am heading there.
5 **Would you mind** if I left a little early today?	(A) Of course not. (B) It's not my concern.

字彙 **budget** 預算　**turn down** 將（音量）調小　**drop . . . off** 將……捎帶至（某地）
head 向（特定方向）出發

請聆聽下列單字和片語，並跟著唸唸看。🎧101

application form	申請表	fill out	填寫（表格、申請表等）
apply for	申請、應徵	financial report	財務報表
available	（人）有空的、（物）可用的、（物）可得到的	M&A (= Mergers and Acquisitions)	併購
be busy with	忙於……	mind	介意
drawer	抽屜	unreal	不真實的、無法相信的

STEP 3　聽寫練習

先聆聽問句和答句，完成句子填空。接著再選出所有適當的回答。🎧102

1 Could you please ＿＿＿＿＿ this ＿＿＿＿＿＿？

(A) The job is ＿＿＿＿＿．

(B) I will ＿＿＿＿＿．

(C) I've ＿＿＿＿＿ it.

2 Do you ＿＿＿＿＿ the ＿＿＿＿＿？

(A) Of course not. ＿＿＿＿＿？

(B) I don't think ＿＿＿＿＿．

(C) It's time to ＿＿＿＿＿．

3 ＿＿＿＿＿ a taxi to take me to the airport?

(A) No, thanks. ＿＿＿＿＿．

(B) Sure. ＿＿＿＿＿ it?

(C) The ＿＿＿＿＿ was ＿＿＿＿＿．

4 ＿＿＿＿＿ help me with this ＿＿＿＿＿？

(A) I am busy ＿＿＿＿＿．

(B) Sorry. I don't ＿＿＿＿＿．

(C) ＿＿＿＿＿ it.

5 ＿＿＿＿＿ find the M&A file?

(A) I ＿＿＿＿＿. No, thanks.

(B) ＿＿＿＿＿．

(C) I think I ＿＿＿＿＿．

6 ＿＿＿＿＿ the air conditioner?

(A) ＿＿＿＿＿, I do. It's ＿＿＿＿＿ in ＿＿＿＿＿．

(B) I ＿＿＿＿＿．

(C) They will ＿＿＿＿＿．

實戰演練 Practice Test

(A) 聆聽問句和選項，並選出最適當的回答。 103

1　Mark your answer on your answer sheet.　　　(A)　(B)　(C)

2　Mark your answer on your answer sheet.　　　(A)　(B)　(C)

3　Mark your answer on your answer sheet.　　　(A)　(B)　(C)

4　Mark your answer on your answer sheet.　　　(A)　(B)　(C)

5　Mark your answer on your answer sheet.　　　(A)　(B)　(C)

6　Mark your answer on your answer sheet.　　　(A)　(B)　(C)

7　Mark your answer on your answer sheet.　　　(A)　(B)　(C)

8　Mark your answer on your answer sheet.　　　(A)　(B)　(C)

9　Mark your answer on your answer sheet.　　　(A)　(B)　(C)

10　Mark your answer on your answer sheet.　　　(A)　(B)　(C)

1 _____ please _____
of the survey for the manager?

(A) I will do it _____ the _____.

(B) The _____ is
_____ fine.

(C) _____.

2 _____ please _____
over to Mr. Brown?

(A) Sure. I _____.

(B) It's _____.

(C) I _____ a hand.

3 _____ a break
before _____?

(A) So far, _____.

(B) _____ a great idea.

(C) _____ has been _____.

4 _____ at the gas
station before we _____
_____?

(A) _____, please.

(B) I _____ you.

(C) I think we _____ it.

5 Could you _____
_____ before you leave?

(A) Sorry. _____.

(B) I _____ , but I can't
guarantee anything.

(C) I can't _____.

6 Do you think you could _____
_____?

(A) Sure. I _____ it.

(B) He _____ me _____.

(C) Sorry. _____.

7 _____ Jack's
_____ for next week?

(A) _____ I didn't _____.

(B) I will _____.

(C) _____ about it.

8 _____ a few days _____
and relax?

(A) I didn't _____.

(B) I'd _____.

(C) The _____.

9 _____ me with the
inventory?

(A) I _____ long hours.

(B) _____.

(C) Sure. I _____.

10 _____
at the opening ceremony?

(A) Sorry, but _____ this time.

(B) He is _____.

(C) _____.

09 直述句

提出問題點

STEP 1 題型演練

A 聆聽問句，並選出適當的回答。 105

Q I can't reach the bottle on the top shelf.
(A) Do you want me to get it for you?
(B) The books are on the bottom shelf.
(C) I should drink it all.

> **Q.** 我拿不到放在最上層架子上的瓶子。
> (A) 要我幫你拿嗎？
> (B) 書放在最下層的架子上。
> (C) 我應該全部喝掉。
> 答案 (A)

▶ 請務必掌握直述句中提及的問題點。針對「手拿不到架上東西」的問題點，(A) 提出解決方式「Do you want me to get it for you?」（要我幫你拿嗎？），故為正確答案。

解題重點

- 題目以直述句提出問題點時，有各式各樣的回答方式，難以事先預測答案。因此，解題重點在於確切掌握問題點所在。
  Q Our sales are **going down.**〔提出問題點〕我們的業績正在下滑中。
  A I've heard about that, too.〔同意〕我也聽說了。
  A Do you know the reason?〔提問〕你知道原因嗎？
  A We should do some promotional events.〔解決方式〕我們應該舉辦一些促銷活動。
  A I am sure next quarter will be better.〔安慰〕我相信下一季會更好。

B 聽完問句和答句後，選出相對應的回答。 106

1 We are **running out of gas**.	(A) My car broke down. (B) Where is the nearest gas station?
2 I **can't turn on** this projector.	(A) Try the red button. (B) The picture is not clear.
3 The numbers in the report are **not accurate**.	(A) Mr. Lee will proofread it later. (B) Thank you for your help.
4 My flight **has been delayed** by 8 hours.	(A) The airport was too crowded. (B) Why don't you try a different flight?
5 My laptop is **not working**.	(A) Isn't it a new one? (B) How did it go?

字彙 **run out of** 用完……　**break down** 故障　**turn on** 打開（電器）　**accurate** 正確的、精確的
delay 延誤、延遲　**crowded** 擁擠的　**work**（機器等）運轉

請聆聽下列單字及片語，並跟著唸唸看。 🎧107

brochure	小冊子、資料手冊	personnel files	人事檔案
budget	預算	pharmacy	藥局
confidential	機密的	repairman	維修人員
missing	丟失的、找不到的	safe	保險箱
out of order	故障的	shipment	貨物配送
outdated	過時的	short of	缺少……的

STEP 3 聽寫練習

先聆聽問句和答句，完成句子填空。接著再選出所有適當的回答。 🎧108

1 The coffee maker is _____.

   (A) It might _____.

   (B) Did you _____?

   (C) The shipment is delayed.

2 I don't think I can _____ _____ today.

   (A) We are _____.

   (B) Is it _____?

   (C) I'd love to help you.

3 I didn't realize that the _____ _____ today.

   (A) Dr. Wilson is _____.

   (B) You'd better _____.

   (C) The one on Maple Street is open.

4 I can't find the _____.

   (A) Nancy was _____ yesterday.

   (B) Have you _____?

   (C) The _____.

5 This product brochure _____.

   (A) Let's _____.

   (B) The marketing team is _____.

   (C) I like the design.

6 The photocopier _____ again.

   (A) I think we _____.

   (B) The report is on your desk.

   (C) Do you want me _____?

表達消息或意見

STEP 1 **題型演練**

Ⓐ 聆聽問句，並選出適當的回答。 🎧109

Q I thought the digital marketing program was really helpful.

(A) I can help you with that.

(B) I completely agree with you.

(C) Of course. You can borrow mine.

Q. 我認為那門數位行銷課程真的很有幫助。

(A) 我可以幫你做那個。

(B) 我完全同意你的看法。

(C) 當然好，你可以借我的去用。

答案 (B)

▶ 本題使用直述句，針對數位行銷課程表達自己的意見。對此，(B) 回答「I completely agree with you.」（我完全同意你的看法。），表示同意對方意見，故為最適當的回答。

🗒 解題重點

● 以直述句表達客觀的事實或消息。

Q Mr. Lee **will be transferred** to headquarters. 李先生將轉調到總公司。

A Good for him. 真棒。

A Has it already been decided? 已經決定了嗎？

● 以直述句表達本人的意見。

Q We **should go** to the art exhibition that opened yesterday.
我們應該去一下昨天開幕的藝術展。

A **Let's go** this Friday. 我們這週五去吧。

A Sorry. I'm **not interested** in art. 抱歉，我對藝術沒興趣。

Ⓑ 聽完問句和答句後，選出相對應的回答。 🎧110

1 The renovation work will **start** in June.	(A) It is under construction. (B) Wasn't it supposed to start in May?
2 I am calling to **cancel** my trip to Italy.	(A) Are you going to reschedule it? (B) He is on vacation.
3 You **should take a walk** instead of staying indoors.	(A) Yes, I need some fresh air. (B) I was late for work today.
4 The software has been **upgraded** to a new version.	(A) A few days ago. (B) Isn't that great?
5 I will **book** a hotel room and a flight later today.	(A) It was really fun. (B) Where are you going?

字彙 renovation work 整修工作　construction 建造、施工　reschedule 重新安排……的時間
instead of 代替……　book 預訂、預約

請聆聽下列單字及片語，並跟著唸唸看。 🎧111

borrow	借入	look for	尋找
construction site	候選人、應徵者	protective helmet	安全帽
candidate	候選人、應徵者	protective helmet	安全帽
construction site	建築工地	put off	延後、拖延
go well	進展順利	put on	穿上、戴上（衣物）
impressive	令人印象深刻的	quarterly	季的
interview	面試	reliable	可信賴的、可靠的

STEP 3　聽寫練習

先聆聽問句和答句，完成句子填空。接著再選出所有適當的回答。 🎧112

1　I think Mr. Harris is _____ for the project.

　(A) My interview _____.

　(B) Yes, he is _____.

　(C) Only two candidates.

2　You should _____ at the construction site.

　(A) _____ get one?

　(B) Then I have to _____.

　(C) I am wearing a hat.

3　I _____ on your desk.

　(A) Thanks. I will check it later.

　(B) I hope _____.

　(C) I _____.

4　I heard that we are all _____ at the end of this month.

　(A) I am _____ the bank.

　(B) I _____ that.

　(C) Do you know _____?

5　The _____ this week.

　(A) Sales are not bad.

　(B) I thought it was last week.

　(C) It was _____.

6　I think we should _____.

　(A) I _____.

　(B) We are _____.

　(C) _____ next Friday then?

實戰演練 *Practice Test*

Ⓐ 聆聽問句和選項，並選出最適當的回答。 113

1 Mark your answer on your answer sheet.   (A)   (B)   (C)

2 Mark your answer on your answer sheet.   (A)   (B)   (C)

3 Mark your answer on your answer sheet.   (A)   (B)   (C)

4 Mark your answer on your answer sheet.   (A)   (B)   (C)

5 Mark your answer on your answer sheet.   (A)   (B)   (C)

6 Mark your answer on your answer sheet.   (A)   (B)   (C)

7 Mark your answer on your answer sheet.   (A)   (B)   (C)

8 Mark your answer on your answer sheet.   (A)   (B)   (C)

9 Mark your answer on your answer sheet.   (A)   (B)   (C)

10 Mark your answer on your answer sheet.   (A)   (B)   (C)

1 These new computers are _____
   _____ .

   (A) They really are.

   (B) Sorry. I already had some.

   (C) We _____ the software.

2 I want to take the afternoon flight to
   Sydney.

   (A) For _____ .

   (B) _____ the morning one?

   (C) It was a short trip.

3 I _____ to work
   properly.

   (A) Does it need _____ ?

   (B) The other supplier has better paper.

   (C) I _____ at 10
       o'clock.

4 Professor Garcia _____
   on Thursday morning.

   (A) I _____ before.

   (B) _____ Tuesday morning?

   (C) The classroom is _____ .

5 I don't know _____ this
   new fax machine.

   (A) I can join you.

   (B) No, I _____
       well.

   (C) I _____ somewhere.

6 I _____ for the
   plastic containers we use.

   (A) Are the _____ ?

   (B) _____ , please.

   (C) We bought a lot of bottles.

7 I _____
   as vice president.

   (A) It was last Friday.

   (B) Please _____ .

   (C) I believe it was Ms. White.

8 I just found out that _____
   _____ .

   (A) Yes, we repaired it yesterday.

   (B) It is _____ .

   (C) Did you _____ ?

9 I'd like to _____ , please.

   (A) No worries.

   (B) I _____ .

   (C) When do you want to _____ ?

10 We _____ the outdoor
   concert.

   (A) A rock music festival.

   (B) I think it is too late.

   (C) Yes, I _____ .

A 選出正確的中文意思。

1　cannot afford to　　　　(A) 負擔不起……　　(B) 聯絡不到……
2　sign up for　　　　　　(A) 放棄　　　　　　(B) 報名參加
3　sales representative　　(A) 業務代表　　　　(B) 業務機密
4　sales figures　　　　　(A) 銷售數字　　　　(B) 銷售戰略
5　call in sick　　　　　　(A) 住院　　　　　　(B) 打電話請病假

B 圈選出與中文意思相符的單字。

1　季報告這週五要交。

→ The quarterly report is (due / expiration) this Friday.

2　我不知道會議將會在哪裡舉行。

→ I have no idea where the conference will be (held / installed).

3　我找不到機密文件放在哪裡。

→ I cannot find where the (complicated / confidential) documents are.

4　你可以付現或刷卡。

→ You can pay (in cash / by cash) or by credit card.

5　我認為帕克先生是這個職位的最佳人選。

→ I think Mr. Park is the perfect (candidate / resident) for this position.

C 將括號內的單字按正確的順序排列組合成句子。

1　The manager said we _____ next month.
(get / are / to / going / a bonus)

經理說，我們下個月會有獎金。

2　Do you _____ for a living?
(to / he / know / happen / what / does)

你知道他是做什麼工作維持生計的嗎？

3　Do you _____ or can you go alone?
(me / want / go / with / you / to)

你想要我和你一起去，還是你可以自己去？

4　_____ be at the meeting?
(you / to / aren't / supposed)

你不是應該在開會嗎？

5　Would you _____ to the airport?
(me / like / to / take / you)

要不要我載你去機場？

PART 3

簡短對話
Short Conversations

01 會議／活動

STEP 1 題型演練

A 先看過題目，再聆聽對話，並選出正確答案。 🎧 115

W Let's start today's meeting by discussing the new web page redesign. What do you think of the sample website?	女 我們開始今天的會議，先來討論網頁的新設計吧。你們覺得網站初樣如何？
M1 I think it looks good, but I noticed a small problem. Our old logo looks kind of bad on the new website.	男 1 我覺得看起來還不錯，但我注意到一個小問題，就是新的網站和我們原本的公司商標看起來不搭。
M2 I agree. I think we should change the logo to reflect our new look and design.	男 2 同意。我認為我們應該改一下公司商標，才能反映我們的新風貌和新設計。
W Hmm . . . I'll get a hold of the marketing team and find out what we can do.	女 嗯……我會再聯絡行銷團隊，看能不能找出什麼我們可以做的。

Q What will the woman most likely do next?	**Q.** 女子接下來最有可能怎麼做？
(A) Change the company logo	(A) 修改公司商標
(B) Ask for new logo ideas	(B) 詢問新商標的點子
(C) Contact the Marketing Department	(C) 聯絡行銷部門
(D) Update the new website	(D) 將新網站更新
	答案 (C)

▶ 本題詢問女子下一步將做的事。碰上這類問題時，通常可以從對話最後幾句找出答題相關線索。女子在最後提到要「聯絡」（get a hold of）行銷團隊，因此答案為 (C)。「get a hold of」可與單字 contact 替換使用。

🖹 解題重點

- 與會議相關的對話情境，有討論業務或日程、檢視目前工作進度等。
- 與活動相關的對話情境，有宣傳活動、準備研討會等活動、教育培訓等。

B 再聽一遍上面的對話，並針對題目選出適當的答案。 🎧 116

1 What are the speakers mainly talking about?

(A) A new website

(B) Marketing strategies

(C) A fault in a product

2 What problem are the speakers discussing?

(A) A lack of funds

(B) A mismatch with a company logo

(C) The bad design of a new logo

STEP 2　常考用法

Ⓐ 聆聽下列單字、片語及句型,並跟著唸唸看。🎧117

1 會議相關用語

Let's get started 我們開始吧
Let's start by -ing 我們從……開始吧
I would like to start by -ing 我想要從……開始
go over today's agenda 重述一次今日的議程
detailed discussion 詳細的討論
make time to meet 找時間見面
call a meeting 召開會議
call off a meeting 取消會議
What do you think . . . ? 你（們）覺得……如何？
I think we should . . . 我認為我們應該……
come up with ideas 想出點子
make it to a meeting 參加會議

2 活動相關用語

board meeting 董事會
shareholder's meeting 股東會
convention 大會
conference 研討會、會議
job fair 公開徵才活動
a location/venue 地點／會場
fundraising party 募款餐會
retirement party 退休歡送會
company banquet 公司宴會
upcoming events 近期活動
sign up for 報名參加
host an event 舉辦活動

Ⓑ 聆聽下面的句子,並完成填空。🎧118

1　I am afraid I might have to _____ .

　　我恐怕得取消這場會議。

2　_____ hire more sales clerks.

　　我認為我們應增聘業務員。

3　I was told that the _____ will no longer _____ .

　　我聽說會議中心不再舉辦這些活動。

4　If you would like to _____ , you should _____ it as soon as possible.

　　你如果想參加那場研討會,就應該盡快報名。

5　We should _____ some recommendations to _____ .

　　我們必須想出一些建議來提高銷售量。

6　Let me _____ before we start.

　　在我們開始之前,我先重述一次今日的議程。

Ⓐ 聆聽對話後，針對題目選出適當的答案。 🎧119

1 What does the man likely mean when he says, "That's hard to say"?

(A) That information is a secret.

(B) He doesn't want to tell the woman.

(C) He will let the woman know by email.

(D) He is not sure right now.

字彙 take care of 處理　construction 建造
permit 許可證、執照　major 重大的
delay 延誤　timeline 時程

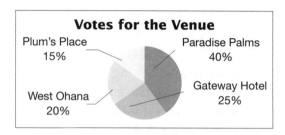

Votes for the Venue

Plum's Place 15%　Paradise Palms 40%
West Ohana 20%　Gateway Hotel 25%

2 Look at the graphic. Where are the speakers likely to have the event?

(A) Paradise Palms

(B) Gateway Hotel

(C) West Ohana

(D) Plum's Place

Ⓑ 再聽一遍對話內容，並完成句子填空。 🎧120

1

M　Well, I think _____ we need to take care of today. Do you have any other questions?

W　I don't think so. Oh, actually, _____. I want to know when the Frederick Building project will be finished.

M　_____. We've had some problems getting a few required _____ _____, so there have been some _____.

W　I see. Well, if you get a _____ for the project, please let me know.

2

M　So, Sharon, did you _____ of the survey about _____ for the _____?

W　I did. Here are the results. _____, Paradise Palms got _____.

M　But do you know what? I _____ from them, and they said they are _____ of our party.

W　Oh, no. Our employees really want that place. What should we do?

M　We should _____ have the party _____.

W　Yeah, I _____. I will _____ and _____ before the end of the day.

Ⓐ 聆聽下面的對話，並選出正確答案。 121

1 What problem does the company have?

(A) It does not have enough cell phone accessories.

(B) It is not selling enough cell phone accessories.

(C) Customers have complained about its cell phone options.

(D) No one wants to sell cell phone accessories.

2 What does the woman likely mean when she says, "You have a point there"?

(A) She agrees with the man's opinion.

(B) She is not so sure about the suggestion.

(C) The men should think about the idea more.

(D) The men should start from the beginning.

3 What does the woman say she will do?

(A) Sell more cell phone accessories

(B) Research the newest phone models

(C) Develop new accessory package ideas

(D) Move to the sales floor

4 Where do the speakers most likely work?

(A) On a sales floor

(B) At a university

(C) At a construction company

(D) At a hotel

5 What are the speakers mainly discussing?

(A) Their next meeting schedule

(B) A workplace policy change

(C) Office renovations

(D) A newly hired faculty member

6 What is the man most likely going to do next?

(A) Call Dr. Hall

(B) Email his flight details

(C) Contact the new professor

(D) Prepare the new office

B 再聽一遍對話內容，並完成句子填空。 🎧 122

[1-3]

M1 _____. The first thing we need to discuss is our _____ _____. Does anyone have any ideas?

M2 I think _____ sales if we _____ that include accessories when you buy a new phone.

W _____. Right now, the packages are really limited, and most customers aren't interested in them. I think we need more options for them.

M1 I like that idea. Suki, can you work with the sales team _____ some new package ideas?

W Sure. I will _____ that we can discuss at _____ _____.

[4-6]

W _____ to meet with me today. We have so much to do to prepare _____.

M Of course. _____ for him to use yet?

W Yes, there is a _____ in the humanities building, so I will _____ this week. But _____ from the airport when he arrives. Do you think Dr. Hall _____ it?

M I'm not sure, but I can ask her. _____ his flight details?

W Sure, I'll _____. When can you talk with Dr. Hall?

M Actually, let me _____ right now.

STEP 1 題型演練

A 先看過題目，再聆聽對話，並選出正確答案。 🎧123

M Hello, Mia. Did you make a reservation for dinner at the Italian restaurant we talked about? Our partners from Brazil will be here tomorrow, so I want to make sure everything is ready.

W Oh, didn't Mr. Hock tell you? That restaurant doesn't have any tables available, so I booked a table at the Indian restaurant down the road.

M No, I didn't know that. I'm glad I asked. Can you email me the reservation details when you have a moment?

W Of course. I'll send them to you right away.

男 哈囉，米亞。我們說的那家義大利餐廳，你訂好晚餐的位子了嗎？我們的巴西合作夥伴明天就會來，我想確定一下是不是一切都準備就緒了。

女 噢，霍克先生沒跟你說嗎？那家餐廳沒空位了，所以我訂了同一條街上的印度餐廳。

男 沒有耶，我不知道，還好我有問。那可以請你有空時把訂位資訊用電子郵件寄給我嗎？

女 當然沒問題，我馬上就寄給你。

Q Why did the man call the woman?

(A) To check on the details of an arrangement

(B) To invite her out to dinner

(C) To contact their business partners

(D) To deliver a message to Mr. Hock

Q. 男子為什麼打電話給女子？

(A) 為了確認某項安排的細節

(B) 為了邀她共進晚餐

(C) 為了聯絡他們的商業夥伴

(D) 為了傳訊息給霍克先生

答案 (A)

▶ 本題詢問男子打電話的目的。對話一開始便出現目的，男子詢問是否有預約晚餐的餐廳，因此答案為 (A) To check on the details of an arrangement（確認某項安排的細節）。

解題重點

- 對話主題與業務或日程有關時，經常會出現詢問主旨或目的的考題，因此請務必專心聽清楚對話的主旨。

B 再聽一遍上面的對話，並針對題目選出適當的答案。 🎧124

1 Where will the dinner happen?

(A) At an Italian restaurant

(B) At an Indian restaurant

(C) At a Chinese restaurant

2 What will the woman do next?

(A) She will email the man.

(B) She will contact Mr. Hock.

(C) She will book a table.

A 聆聽下列單字及片語，並跟著唸唸看。 🎧125

1 業務相關用語

quarterly report 季報告
place an order 下訂單
assign a task 指派任務
negotiate a contract 磋商合約
review records 審閱紀錄
official answer 官方答覆
file a request 提出要求
get approval 取得許可
receive reimbursement 收到賠償款／報銷款
challenging task 有挑戰性的任務
do paperwork 處理文書業務
tied up with work 忙著工作、因工作無法脫身
work overtime 加班、超時工作

2 日程相關用語

get in touch with 和……聯絡上
annual event 年度活動
have a day off 休一天假
coordinate an event 策劃活動
run behind 落後、遲到
meet a deadline 趕截止期限
due today 今天截止
extension on a report 延後交報告的時間
put off an event 延後活動
call off a trip 取消旅行
reschedule a meeting 重新安排會議時間
behind schedule 進度落後
be available
（人）有空、（物）可用、（物）可得到

B 聆聽下面的句子，並完成填空。 🎧126

1 If you _____ , you _____ in advance.
　若你想休一天假，就必須事先取得許可。

2 I wonder if I can _____ .
　我想知道我可不可以延後繳交預算報告。

3 Management has decided to _____ .
　高層決定延後公司宴會。

4 I am _____ for my travel expenses.
　我打電話來，是為了我的差旅費報銷一事。

5 We have to _____ for this Saturday.
　我們必須取消這週六安排的戶外活動。

6 Mr. Smith on the management team is _____ .
　經營團隊的史密斯先生正在審閱安全紀錄。

STEP 3 聽寫練習

Ⓐ 聆聽對話後，針對題目選出適當的答案。 🎧 127

1 What will the woman most likely do next?

(A) Call the Marketing Department

(B) Write the quarterly report

(C) Visit the Marketing Department

(D) Help Jim with his work

2 What does the woman imply when she says, "I think that should be okay"?

(A) The man doesn't have to do any extra work.

(B) The man can extend a deadline on a project.

(C) The man can apply for a transfer.

(D) The man will be able to get a day off.

字彙 **quarterly** 季的
this time of year 每年的這個時候
stop by 順路過去

字彙 **wonder** 想知道
extend a deadline 延長截止期限
transfer 轉調

Ⓑ 再聽一遍對話內容，並完成句子填空。 🎧 128

1

W   Hey, Jim, have you _____ from the Marketing Department yet? They told me they would be ready by today, but I _____

_____ .

M   No, I haven't heard anything either. Maybe they are _____ schedule. I know they are busy this time of year. Do you want me to _____

_____ ?

W   That's all right. I'm _____ now, so I'll just _____ . Do you need anything else from them?

M   I don't think so. Thanks anyway.

2

M   Ms. Carter, I wonder if I can _____ . Do you think that would be possible?

W   Next Monday? Yeah, I think that should be okay. Did you _____

_____ on the digital scheduling system?

M   Not yet. I wanted to check with you first _____ .

W   Okay, well, make sure you file your request _____ so that I can _____ .

M   That sounds good. Thanks, Ms. Carter.

A 聆聽下面的對話，並選出正確答案。 🎧 129

TIME	ROOM #	SEATING CAPACITY
2 P.M.	105	8
	106	10
	107	12
	108	6

1 What are the speakers discussing?

(A) Giving a loan to a customer

(B) Opening an account

(C) Reserving a conference room

(D) Contacting a business client

2 What does the man say he will do?

(A) Cancel the meeting

(B) Send the woman the room information

(C) Join the meeting

(D) Train the new tellers

3 Look at the graphic. In which room will the woman have her meeting?

(A) Room 105

(B) Room 106

(C) Room 107

(D) Room 108

4 Where did the speakers most likely work?

(A) At a bank

(B) At a travel agency

(C) At a law firm

(D) At a moving company

5 What did the woman offer the man?

(A) A promotion

(B) A new office

(C) A trip abroad

(D) More vacation time

6 What does the man mean when he says, "I don't know what to say"?

(A) He is confused.

(B) He is surprised.

(C) He is not familiar with the topic.

(D) He cannot help right now.

B 再聽一遍對話內容，並完成句子填空。 🎧 130

[1-3]

W James, I have a client coming this afternoon _____.
He has all of his _____, so it's a very
important meeting. Can you book Room 105 at 2 P.M. for me, please?

M Room 105? That's where the new teller training will be happening this
afternoon. Do you _____?

W Oh, yes, that would be great. Could you _____?

M Yeah, it looks like _____ at 2 P.M. It's
_____ at that time. I'll _____.

W Perfect. Thank you so much.

[4-6]

W Hi, Hans. I _____ for Globi Technology.
You did an excellent job.

M Thanks. I really _____ on their travel plans.

W How would you feel about _____? I think that
you would do a wonderful job _____.

M Wow, do you really think so? I don't know _____. That would be
_____ for me.

W Well, think about it over the weekend, and we can _____
next Monday.

03 人事／聘用

Ⓐ 先看過題目，再聆聽對話，並選出正確答案。🎧 131

W1 Hey, Sasha. It's Mina. I can't log into my employee page on the HR website. Can you reset my password for me?	女1 嗨，莎夏，我是米娜。我登不進去人資網站的員工頁面。你可以幫我重設一下密碼嗎？
W2 No problem. That has been happening a lot since the IT Department updated our servers. What's your employee ID number?	女2 沒問題，這個情形在資訊科技部幫我們更新伺服器後，已經發生過好幾次了。你的員工編號是多少？
W1 Thanks. It's 501563.	女1 謝謝，是 501563。
W2 Okay, I sent you an email with instructions. Just follow the link and enter your information. It should only take a couple minutes.	女2 好，我寄了一封電子郵件說明到你的信箱，只要依照連結指示並輸入你的資料就行了。應該不會花你幾分鐘。

Q What information does Sasha ask for?	Q. 莎夏要求什麼資訊？
(A) A website password	(A) 網站密碼
(B) An employee ID number	(B) 員工編號
(C) An email address	(C) 電子郵件地址
(D) A website URL	(D) 網站網址
	答案 (B)

▶ 本題詢問女子要求什麼資訊。Sasha（莎夏）在對話中段詢問「What's your employee ID number?」，由此便能輕鬆找出答案。值得留意的是，雖然文中有提及 email、website、password 等單字，但是千萬不要因此誤選答案。

🗒 解題重點

- 與人事和聘用相關的對話情境，有僱用員工（hiring）、升遷（promotion）、福利（welfare）、退休（retirement）等。
- 若能熟記愈多與人事和聘用有關的單字，愈有助於理解對話內容。

Ⓑ 再聽一遍上面的對話，並針對題目選出適當的答案。🎧 132

1 What problem does Mina mention?
   (A) She forgot her password.
   (B) She cannot access the HR website.
   (C) She cannot update her website.

2 Where does Sasha most likely work?
   (A) In the HR Department
   (B) In the Technology Department
   (C) In the Accounting Department

STEP 2　常考用法

Ⓐ 聆聽下列單字及片語，並跟著唸唸看。 🎧 133

1 人事相關用語

HR (= Human Resources) 人資（部）
employee ID number 員工編號
Personnel Department 人事部
performance evaluation 績效評估
get a promotion 升職、得到提拔
get promoted 升職、得到提拔
sick leave 病假
paycheck 薪資單
commission 佣金、手續費
employee training 員工訓練
pay raise 加薪
retire 退休
renew a contract 續簽合約
take a day off 休一天假

2 聘用相關用語

application 應徵、申請、申請表
apply for a position 應徵工作
applicant 應徵者
candidate 候選人、應徵者
résumé 履歷
recruit new staff 招聘新人
potential employee 潛在員工、招聘對象
job opening 職缺
information packet（給新進員工的）資料包
cover letter 求職信
qualifications 資格、合格條件
conduct an interview（對應徵者）面試

Ⓑ 聆聽下面的句子，並完成填空。 🎧 134

1 Do you think I could _____ next week?
　你覺得我下週能休一天假嗎？

2 I am calling to ask you about the _____ advertised on your website.
　我打來是想問您有關貴公司網站上刊登的職缺一事。

3 We are going to have a _____ for _____ who are interested in our company.
　我們將舉行公開徵才活動，招聘對我們公司感興趣的潛在對象。

4 Since our products are in such high demand, we need to _____ for next year.
　由於我們的產品需求大，所以必須招募新人以備明年之需。

5 If you would like to _____ the _____ , please submit your résumé along with a _____ .
　你如果想應徵該職位，請提供你的履歷並附上求職信。

6 It's not going to be easy to _____ if your _____ is not satisfactory.
　如果你的績效不符合要求，會不太容易續約。

Ⓐ 聆聽對話後，針對題目選出適當的答案。 🎧135

1 What is going to happen next Monday?

(A) They will hire a new employee.

(B) The speakers are going to look at the résumés together.

(C) The woman will send the résumés to the man.

(D) The speakers will contact potential employees.

> 字彙 applicant 應徵者　position 職位
> popularity 詢問度
> by the end of this week
> 週末放假前、週五下班以前
> go over 仔細查看

2 What department do the speakers most likely work in?

(A) Human Resources

(B) Marketing

(C) Accounting

(D) Product Development

> 字彙 intern 實習生
> be scheduled to 表定……、被安排……
> info packet (= information packet)
> （給新進員工的）資料包
> make sure 確認

Ⓑ 再聽一遍對話內容，並完成句子填空。 🎧136

1

M _____ you _____ the _____ for the _____? I sent them to your office last week.

W I started, but I _____. There was a lot of interest in the position, so it's _____ than expected.

M Yeah, I noticed that there were a lot _____ than the last time. I'm happy about _____.

W It's great. I should be _____, so let's _____ next Monday.

M Perfect. See you then.

2

W What time will the _____ on Monday?

M The orientation _____ at 9 A.M. Have you finished _____ _____ yet?

W Not quite, but they will be _____. Do you _____ _____ how many interns are coming?

M _____, so _____ enough packets _____.

W Will do. Thanks, Barry.

Ⓐ 聆聽下面的對話，並選出正確答案。🎧 137

1 Why is the man visiting this office?

(A) He lost his paycheck.

(B) He did not receive proper pay.

(C) He needs extra money.

(D) He wants to edit some personal information.

POSITION	OPENINGS	Department
Web Page Designer	2	Online Management
Programmer	4	Computer Development
Product R/D	2	R&D
Floor Manager	1	Sales

4 Why is the man calling?

(A) To cancel an application

(B) To learn about an application procedure

(C) To apply for a position

(D) To find out a website address

2 Why does the woman say, "You have to be kidding"?

(A) To accuse the man of lying

(B) To ask the man to come back later

(C) To tell the man to stop joking

(D) To show that she is shocked

5 When is the application deadline?

(A) June 1

(B) June 20

(C) July 15

(D) July 20

3 What will happen on Wednesday?

(A) The man will be paid properly.

(B) The woman will contact the man again.

(C) The man will return to the office.

(D) The woman will process the man's request.

6 Look at the graphic. Which department is the man interested in a position in?

(A) Online Management

(B) Computer Development

(C) R&D

(D) Sales

[1-3]

M   Excue me. I'm _____, but I think there was a
    mistake _____. _____ wasn't
    included.

W   You _____. You're _____ who has had this
    problem _____. Do you have your _____ with
    you?

M   Oh, really? Yes, here is my info. How long _____
    the problem?

W   Let's see. Yes, _____. _____, and
    you should receive _____.

M   Oh, that's great. Thank you so much.

[4-6]

M   Hello. I'm interested in _____ as a web page
    designer, but I have a question.

W   Of course. Thanks for _____. How can I help
    you?

M   _____ when the starting date for the position is. It says here on
    the website that _____ July 15. I also would like to know when
    the _____ is.

W   Oh, yes, the _____ is July 20. The 15th is for
    programmers and the _____. And all _____
    by June 1. Do you have any other questions?

M   No, _____ I needed to know. Thank you.

W   You're very welcome. Have a great day.

PART 3

04 旅遊／出差

STEP 1 題型演練

A 先看過題目，再聆聽對話，並選出正確答案。 🎧 139

W Eric, have you booked the flight tickets for our trip to Manchester? You need to do that as soon as possible if you haven't.

M Not yet. What date does the conference start? We want to arrive one day early, right?

W Yeah, the event starts on the 12th, so you should book four tickets for the 11th.

M Okay, you can count on me. I'll give the details to you by the end of the day.

女 艾瑞克，你訂好我們去曼徹斯特出差的機票了嗎？如果還沒，你得趕快訂了。

男 還沒。會議是哪一天開始啊？我們要提前一天到，對吧？

女 對啊，活動是 12 日開始，所以你應該訂四張 11 日的票。

男 好，放心交給我吧。我下班前會把詳細資料給你。

Q What event is the woman planning to attend?

(A) An interview
(B) A job fair
(C) A conference
(D) An opening ceremony

Q. 女子打算參加什麼活動？

(A) 面試
(B) 公開徵才活動
(C) 會議
(D) 開幕典禮

答案 (C)

▶ 本題詢問的是相關細節，針對女子欲參加的活動提問。男子詢問會議開始的日期（What date does the conference start?），由此可知女子將要參加會議，因此答案為 (C)。

📖 解題重點

• 對話主題與旅遊或出差有關時，經常會出現詢問預約、準備、確認、使用疑問等相關細節題。作答相關細節題時，請務必於對話播放前讀完題目，以確認聆聽時要將重點放在哪一方面的資訊上。

B 再聽一遍上面的對話，並針對題目選出適當的答案。 🎧 140

1 When does the event start?

(A) On the 11th
(B) On the 12th
(C) On the 13th

2 What does the man mean when he says, "you can count on me"?

(A) He will reserve the tickets.
(B) He is willing to pay for the tickets.
(C) He can accompany the woman.

A 聆聽下列單字及片語，並跟著唸唸看。 🎧 141

1 機場相關用語

direct flight 直飛班機
connecting flight 轉接班機
miss a flight 錯過班機
transfer 轉乘
boarding pass 登機證
a form of identification
身分證件（護照、身分證等）
aisle seat 靠走道的座位
window seat 靠窗的座位
flight attendant 空服員
cabin crew 機組人員
overseas travel 海外旅行
luggage/baggage 行李
carry-on baggage 手提行李
luggage carousel (= baggage claim)
行李領取處
overhead compartment
（機艙座位）上方行李置物櫃
runway 飛機跑道
arrival/departure 抵達／出發

2 旅遊、飯店相關用語

go on a business trip 去出差
leave 休假
check in/out 入住／退房
reserve/book a room 訂（飯店）房間
porter 行李員
wakeup call 叫醒服務
final destination （旅程）最終目的地
itinerary 行程表
unavailable
（人）沒空的、（物）不可用的、（物）不可取得的
travel agency/agent 旅行社／旅行社職員
go sightseeing 去觀光
accommodations 住宿
embassy 大使館
fill out/in a form 填寫表格
jet lag 時差
round trip 往返行程
current exchange 換匯
traveler's check 旅行支票

B 聆聽下面的句子，並完成填空。 🎧 142

1 You cannot leave the country _____ .
您沒有身分證件不能出國。

2 Please _____ under your seat or _____ .
請將您的手提行李放在您座位下面，或上方的置物櫃裡。

3 Would you like _____ or _____ ?
您的座位想要靠走道還是靠窗？

4 Please _____ before landing.
請在飛機降落前填好這張表。

5 I wonder if I can _____ for Saturday night.
我想問我能不能訂兩間這週六晚上的飯店房間。

6 _____ in Jeju are _____ in August.
八月濟州島的住宿全都被訂滿了。

STEP 3　聽寫練習

A 聆聽對話後，針對題目選出適當的答案。🎧143

FRONT

4A	4B		4C	4D
5A	5B	Aisle	5C	5D
6A	6B		6C	6D

BACK

1 Look at the graphic. Where will the woman sit?

(A) 5A　　　　(C) 6A

(B) 5B　　　　(D) 6B

2 What information does the man ask for?

(A) An email address

(B) A name

(C) An invoice number

(D) A conference ID number

> 字彙 **window seat** 靠窗的座位
> **behind** 在……後方
> **flight attendant** 空服員

> 字彙 **sign up for** 報名參加　**exhibition** 展覽
> **take place** 舉行　**register** 登記、註冊
> **registration** 登記、註冊

B 再聽一遍對話內容，並完成句子填空。🎧144

1

W Excuse me, but I think you ＿＿＿＿＿＿＿＿＿＿. My ticket says I'm in 5A, ＿＿＿＿＿＿＿＿＿＿＿＿＿.

M Oh, really? Let me check my ticket. Hmm . . . Oh, I'm so sorry. It says that I'm ＿＿＿＿＿＿＿＿＿＿. That was my mistake.

W That's no problem. I ＿＿＿＿＿＿＿＿＿ with you. ＿＿＿＿＿＿＿ ＿＿＿＿＿ than having you move.

M That's so kind of you. Thank you so much. I'll ＿＿＿＿＿＿＿＿＿＿＿＿.

2

W Hello. ＿＿＿＿＿＿＿＿＿＿ the Las Vegas Technology Exhibition ＿＿＿＿＿＿＿＿＿. My company would like to ＿＿＿＿＿＿＿＿＿.

M Okay. Is this your first time ＿＿＿＿＿＿＿＿＿？

W No, we have had a booth every year for the last 3 years.

M Oh, then registration should be very simple. What name ＿＿＿＿＿＿＿＿＿ ＿＿＿＿＿＿＿ last year? I can ＿＿＿＿＿＿＿＿ to create a new registration for this year.

Ⓐ 聆聽下面的對話，並選出正確答案。 🎧 145

1 What does the man ask for?

(A) A ticket
(B) A form of identification
(C) A boarding pass
(D) A reservation number

2 What does the woman have to do in Tulsa?

(A) Receive a new boarding pass
(B) Pick up her luggage
(C) Request a seat change
(D) Present her passport

3 Where will the woman find her checked bag?

(A) At the Tulsa departing gate
(B) At the Philadelphia airline counter
(C) At the Tulsa baggage claim
(D) At the Philadelphia baggage claim

4 Who most likely are the speakers?

(A) Family members
(B) Hotel employees
(C) Coworkers
(D) Friends

5 What are the speakers going to do tomorrow?

(A) Apply for a job
(B) Check out early
(C) Take a taxi
(D) Attend a meeting

6 What will the man do next?

(A) Speak with a hotel receptionist
(B) Check out of the hotel
(C) Contact a law firm about a meeting
(D) Ask to have his breakfast delivered early

B 再聽一遍對話內容，並完成句子填空。 🎧 146

[1-3]

M   Good afternoon. _____, please?

W   Here you are.

M   What is _____ today? And will you be checking any bags?

W   I'm going to Philadelphia, and, yes, I would like to check this bag, please.

M   Okay. I see _____ in Tulsa. You have to _____ _____ when you get there, so please go to the airline counter as soon as you arrive.

W   I see. Do I need to _____ in Tulsa as well?

M   No, your bag will _____. You _____ area there.

[4-6]

W1   _____ tomorrow? Will we have time to _____ with the partners at the Lakeview Law Firm?

M   We should check out at 12 P.M., so I think we should _____. I'm sure there is a place we can keep them at their office.

W2   Well, why don't we just ask the hotel _____? It would be such a pain to bring our things all the way to the office.

W1   Good idea, Lisa. I don't mind _____. It would be better to leave our bags at the hotel during the meeting.

M   Hmm . . . let's _____. I think we can pay the fee by _____.

A 選出正確的中文意思。

1　shareholder's meeting　　(A) 股東會　　(B) 股息
2　upcoming events　　(A) 近期活動　　(B) 過去活動
3　behind schedule　　(A) 進度落後　　(B) 進度超前
4　performance evaluation　　(A) 績效評估　　(B) 業務輔助
5　get promoted　　(A) 促銷　　(B) 升職

B 圈選出與中文意思相符的單字。

1　我會再聯絡行銷團隊，看能不能找出什麼我們可以做的。
　➡ I will (get a hold of / get the hang of) the marketing team and find out what we can do.

2　你知道最終會來的實習生人數嗎？
　➡ Do you have (the last number / a final number) on how many interns are coming?

3　我想知道應徵截止日期是什麼時候。
　➡ I would like to know when (the completion / the application) deadline is.

4　我下班前會把詳細資料給你。
　➡ I will give you (the features / the details) by the end of the day.

5　您去年是用誰的名義登記的呢？
　➡ What name did you register (from / under) last year?

C 將括號內的單字按正確的順序排列組合成句子。

1　I think we should _____. (clerks / more / hire / sales)
　我認為我們應增聘業務員。

2　Let me _____ before we start. (agenda / over / today's / go)
　在我們開始之前，我先重述一次今日的議程。

3　The restaurant _____ the party.
　(fully / is / of / day / on / the / booked)
　餐廳在派對當天的預約已經滿了。

4　I will _____. (you / away / to / right / them / send)
　我馬上就寄給你。

5　I can _____. (your / off / approve / time)
　我可以批准你休假。

PART 3

05 設施／辦公室用品

STEP 1 題型演練

Ⓐ 先看過題目，再聆聽對話，並選出正確答案。🎧147

M	The copy machine has broken down three times this month. It's starting to become a big problem.
W	Hmm . . . maybe it's time for an upgrade. I'll ask the manager if we have enough money in the budget for a new one.
M	Oh, that would be great. Could you ask if we can get a copier that does color prints?
W	Sure, I'll talk to him at our meeting tomorrow.

男 影印機這個月已經故障三次了。它變成了大麻煩。

女 嗯……也許是時候升級一下影印機了。我會問問看經理我們的預算夠不夠買一台新的。

男 噢，如果可以就太好了。你能問問看我們可不可以買彩色影印機嗎？

女 好啊，我明天開會時跟他談一下。

Q What does the woman suggest?

(A) Moving to a new department

(B) Buying a new copy machine

(C) Calling a repairman

(D) Printing more documents in color

Q. 女子提議怎麼做？

(A) 換到新的部門

(B) 購買新的影印機

(C) 打電話給維修人員

(D) 彩印更多文件

答案 (B)

▶ 本題詢問女子提議的事。第一段對話中，女子說道：「是時候升級一下影印機了」（it's time for an upgrade），接著又提到「買新影印機的預算」（money in the budget for a new one），由此可知女子的提議為 (B)「購買新的影印機」。

📖 解題重點

- 與設施或辦公室用品相關的對話情境，有辦公室內機器出問題、訂購、配送用品、使用或封閉設施等。同時，會以題組的形式提問相關資訊，因此解題關鍵在於作答前得先讀完題目，以確認聆聽的重點要放在哪一方面的資訊上。

Ⓑ 再聽一遍上面的對話，並針對題目選出適當的答案。🎧148

1 What does the woman imply when she says, "it's time for an upgrade"?

(A) The office needs to be improved.

(B) A new copier is needed.

(C) The copier needs to be fixed.

2 What does the woman say she will do?

(A) Send an email

(B) Purchase a new copier

(C) Ask about the budget

A 聆聽下列單字及片語，並跟著唸唸看。 🎧 149

1 設施相關用語

facilities 設施、建築
under construction 興建中、施工中
in operation 營業中
building renovation 建築整修
mechanic 技術人員
technician 技術人員
parking structure 立體停車場
evacuate 疏散
complex 綜合設施、綜合大樓
emergency exit 緊急出口
conference room 會議室
property 房產、地產、建築
spacious 寬敞的
shut down 關門
leak 漏水
premises 房屋、（經營）場所

2 辦公室用品相關用語

break down 故障
upgrade 改善、升級
call a repairman 打電話給維修人員
print documents 列印文件
run out (of) 用完
put an order in for 訂購（商品）
office supply store 辦公用品店
give a refund 退款
instruction manual 使用說明書
express delivery 快遞
out of order 故障
work properly 正常運作

B 聆聽下面的句子，並完成填空。 🎧 150

1 Why don't we stop by the ＿＿＿＿＿＿＿ store on the way to the office? We ran out of printing paper.

我們何不在上班途中去辦公用品店一趟？我們的影印紙用完了。

2 I am going to ＿＿＿＿＿＿＿ more files later this afternoon.

我今天下午會下訂更多文件夾。

3 I don't think we need to ＿＿＿＿＿＿＿ since this is not ＿＿＿＿＿ .

這不急，我想我們不需要用快遞。

4 Let me give you the number in case you want to ＿＿＿＿＿＿＿ .

你可能會想打電話給維修人員，還是把電話號碼給你好了。

5 The ＿＿＿＿＿＿＿ is under ＿＿＿＿＿＿ , so you should move your car to the ＿＿＿＿＿＿＿ .

立體停車場正在整修中，所以您應該把車子移到公共停車場。

6 Smoking is strictly forbidden ＿＿＿＿＿＿＿ .

室內全面嚴禁吸煙。

STEP 3　聽寫練習

Ⓐ 聆聽對話後，針對題目選出適當的答案。🎧151

1 What did Beatrix do earlier?

(A) She came to work early.

(B) She printed some documents.

(C) She cleaned the supply closet.

(D) She bought some envelopes.

字彙 document 文件　envelope 信封
proposal 提案、計畫書　bend 折到
run out 用完
put an order in for 訂購　urgent 緊急的
office supply store 辦公用品店
pay back 還錢

2 According to the man, what decision was recently made?

(A) To begin construction early

(B) To close the south lot

(C) To make a new contract

(D) To rename the parking lot

字彙 construction 施工
be supposed to（被認為）應該……
lot 停車場
be expected to（被）預計……

Ⓑ 再聽一遍對話內容，並完成句子填空。🎧152

1

M　Do we have any more ＿＿＿＿＿＿＿＿＿＿＿＿? I need to send the

new proposal to our team in Montreal, and I don't want to ＿＿＿＿＿＿＿＿

＿＿＿＿＿＿.

W1　Hmm . . . it seems that we ＿＿＿＿＿＿. I'll ＿＿＿＿＿＿＿＿ some

more. ＿＿＿＿＿＿, you can buy some at the ＿＿＿＿＿＿＿＿

down the road, and the company will ＿＿＿＿＿＿.

W2　Actually, I ＿＿＿＿＿＿＿＿＿＿ this morning. They are ＿＿＿＿

＿＿＿＿＿＿ on the first floor.

M　Oh, that's great! ＿＿＿＿＿＿＿＿＿＿, Beatrix.

2

M　Excuse me, ma'am, but I'm afraid ＿＿＿＿＿＿＿＿＿＿. We are going

to ＿＿＿＿＿＿ here this afternoon.

W　Construction? That ＿＿＿＿＿＿＿＿＿＿ until

tomorrow.

M　We just ＿＿＿＿＿＿＿＿＿＿ because of the weather. You'll

have to ＿＿＿＿＿＿＿＿＿＿, unfortunately.

W　Okay, well, thank you for the information. Do you know when the construction

＿＿＿＿＿＿＿＿＿＿?

M　I'm not sure, but I don't expect ＿＿＿＿＿＿＿＿＿＿.

A 聆聽下面的對話，並選出正確答案。 153

1 What is the conversation mainly about?

(A) A new employee

(B) Transferring departments

(C) Equipment for a meeting

(D) Upgrading some facilities

2 According to the man, what can the woman do?

(A) Reserve a conference room for a meeting

(B) Ask an IT employee to prepare some equipment

(C) Take tomorrow off from work

(D) Give the meeting to someone else

3 What is the woman's concern?

(A) She is going to be late for work.

(B) Her boss might be mad at her.

(C) Her meeting might be canceled tomorrow.

(D) She doesn't know how to use some technical equipment.

4 What are the speakers talking about?

(A) The sales figures for this quarter

(B) A new promotion

(C) A temporary change

(D) Workplace responsibilities

5 What does the man ask the woman to do?

(A) Make some signs

(B) Distribute promotional fliers

(C) Call a repairman

(D) Make a phone call

6 What did the man do earlier?

(A) Made some signs about an issue

(B) Informed the employees about a change

(C) Prepared a website to reflect some information

(D) Asked his boss for more information

B 再聽一遍對話內容，並完成句子填空。 🎧154

[1-3]

W Dan, I need _____ for tomorrow's meeting. Are
any of the _____?

M Hmm . . . it looks like all the rooms _____. You _____
one of the _____ and set it up _____.

W That sounds kind of difficult. I've never used _____
before, and _____ that it might not work properly.

M Don't worry. You can ask someone _____ to
help. They can _____ for you. Just call them and
_____.

W Wow, _____ I needed! Thank you so much.

[4-6]

M Tomorrow, the _____ are going to be _____.
Could you _____ to explain that we will _____
the second-floor bathrooms _____?

W Of course. How long _____?

M The repairs should _____, so just explain that the
inconvenience _____.

W Got it. Should we send an email out _____ to _____?

M I already did that this morning, so all the employees should know about it.
Let's just _____ to _____.

06 產品／服務

Ⓐ 先看過題目，再聆聽對話，並選出正確答案。 🎧 155

W Hello, Mr. Wells. I work for *Health and Fitness* magazine. You recently canceled your subscription, and I wonder if I can ask you a few questions about why you did that.	女 威爾斯先生您好，這裡是《健康和健身雜誌》。您最近取消了訂閱服務，不知道方不方便問您幾個問題，請教您取消的原因呢？
M Sure, what would you like to know?	男 好的，您想知道什麼呢？
W First of all, was there a particular reason you decided to discontinue service with us?	女 首先，請問有特殊的理由讓您決定停止使用我們的服務嗎？
M Oh, I was just trying to cut back on expenses.	男 噢，我只是想減少支出罷了。

Q Why did the man cancel his subscription to the magazine? (A) To save money (B) To save time (C) To make a complaint (D) To subscribe to a different one	**Q.** 男子為什麼退訂雜誌？ (A) 為了省錢 (B) 為了省時 (C) 為了投訴 (D) 為了訂閱其他雜誌 答案 (A)

▶ 女子詢問停止訂閱的原因，對此男子回答「cut back on expenses」(減少支出)。此句話可以替換成 (A) To save money (省錢)，故 (A) 為正確答案。

🗈 解題重點

- 與產品或服務相關的對話情境中，經常出現顧客與員工間的對話。主題包含銷售、配送、退款、維修、客訴、諮詢等內容。

Ⓑ 再聽一遍上面的對話，並針對題目選出適當的答案。 🎧 156

1 What kind of business does the woman work for?

(A) Manufacturing
(B) Banking
(C) Publishing

2 Why is the woman calling?

(A) To ask about a cancelation
(B) To ask about a late payment
(C) To ask about a discount

STEP 2　常考用法

A 聆聽下列單字及片語，並跟著唸唸看。 🎧157

① 銷售、配送相關用語

carry an item 有販售某商品
in stock 有庫存
take inventory 盤點存貨
manufacturer 製造商
quality 品質
reliable 可信賴的、可靠的
state-of-the-art machine 先進的機器
handmade 手工的
up-to-date 流行的、最新的
deliver a product 送貨
warehouse 倉庫
shipment 貨物配送
aisle 通道、走道
appliance 電器
goods 商品
storage facility 倉儲設施
pick up 收（件）、拿取
distribute 分發、分配
invoice 出貨明細

② 維修、退款、客訴相關用語

get/receive a refund 取得／收到退款
return a product 退貨
exchange an item 換貨
check a manual 查閱使用手冊
for free 免費
original receipt 收據正本
guarantee 保證書
replace 替換
charge 收費
apologize 道歉
recall 召回
make a complaint 投訴
defective 有瑕疵的
inconvenience 不便
at no extra charge 無額外收費
laundry service 洗衣服務
customer service representative 客服專員

B 聆聽下面的句子，並完成填空。 🎧158

1 You must ＿＿＿＿＿＿＿＿ of the product to ＿＿＿＿＿＿＿＿.
您必須攜帶收據正本，才能取得退款。

2 You can ＿＿＿ ＿＿＿＿＿ a little after 3 P.M.
您下午 3 點過後不久就可以領取禮服。

3 We are truly ＿＿＿＿＿＿＿＿.
對於造成不便，我們十分抱歉。

4 We are afraid that we don't ＿＿＿＿＿＿＿.
很遺憾，我們不提供洗衣服務。

5 I wonder if you ＿＿＿＿＿＿＿ in the store.
我想問您店裡有沒有賣家電。

6 The store ＿＿＿＿＿＿ for these pair of jeans.
這條牛仔褲店家賣 70 美元。

Ⓐ 聆聽對話後，針對題目選出適當的答案。🎧159

1 Why did the man call?

　(A) He wanted to exchange a product.

　(B) He had a problem receiving a refund.

　(C) A store didn't send him a product.

　(D) There was a missing document.

字彙 **refund** 退款、退還　**shop assistant** 店員
receipt 收據　**approve** 核准
delay 延遲

2 What are the speakers talking about?

　(A) Repairing a product

　(B) Designing a logo

　(C) Canceling a purchase

　(D) Changing an order

字彙 **order** 訂單　**take care of** 處理

Ⓑ 再聽一遍對話內容，並完成句子填空。🎧160

1

M Hi. My name is Abel Martin, and I'm calling about ＿＿＿＿＿＿＿ at your store last month. The shop assistant told me that I would ＿＿＿＿＿＿＿ within two weeks, but it ＿＿＿＿＿＿＿.

W I'm sorry to hear that. Do you have ＿＿＿＿＿＿＿ with you?

M Yes, it's 554001.

W Let me see. It looks like your refund request ＿＿＿＿＿＿＿. I'll approve it now. You should receive the refund ＿＿＿＿＿＿＿. I'm very ＿＿＿＿＿＿＿.

M It's no problem.

2

M Hello. This is Jake from Howser Communications. I have ＿＿＿＿＿＿＿ to our print order. ＿＿＿＿＿＿＿?

W Of course. If you email me the document and let me know ＿＿＿＿＿＿＿, I ＿＿＿＿＿＿＿. That is no problem. And please let me know if it is a color or black and white order.

M Okay, I'll ＿＿＿＿＿＿＿ right now. When do you think ＿＿＿＿＿＿＿?

W If you send me the new document right now, I can probably ＿＿＿＿＿＿＿.

A 聆聽下面的對話，並選出正確答案。 161

Plan	Data	Cost per Month
A	500MB	$15
B	1GB	$30
C	2GB	$45
D	5GB	$60

1 Where most likely are the speakers?

(A) At a telecommunications shop

(B) At an accounting firm

(C) At a call center

(D) At an IT conference

2 What does the man want to do?

(A) Upgrade his data service

(B) Cancel his existing phone service

(C) Sign up for a new phone service

(D) Apply for a customer service job

3 Look at the graphic. How much will the man pay per month for his new plan?

(A) $15

(B) $30

(C) $45

(D) $60

4 Why does the woman call?

(A) She is lost.

(B) She needs help with her copy machine.

(C) She is going to be late.

(D) She wants to cancel her appointment.

5 What problem does the woman mention?

(A) A device is out of order.

(B) She forgot about an appointment.

(C) Her car has broken down.

(D) The road traffic is heavy.

6 What does the man tell the woman?

(A) How to enter a building

(B) Where a copy machine is

(C) What is wrong with a copy machine

(D) What time he will be there

[1-3]

M   Hi. I'm _____. Can you show me _____
_____ for plans that include data?

W   Certainly. As you can see on this chart, we have _____.
The cost _____. Our 2-gigabyte plan is _____
_____ right now.

M   Hmm . . . well . . . I need at least 3 gigabytes per month, so I _____
_____.

W   Well, you can see here that we have one plan with more than 3 gigabytes.
_____?

M   That sounds perfect. Can I _____ today?

W   Absolutely. _____ for you to _____, and
we can _____ right away.

[4-6]

W   Hello. This is Adela from Davis Repairs. I am _____
to repair your copy machine, but I think I'll be late because of the traffic jam.

M   Oh, I'm sorry to hear that, but _____. What
time _____?

W   Well, I _____ by 3 P.M., but I think I will arrive a little
after 4 P.M. Is that all right?

M   Yes, it's no problem. When you arrive, please _____,
and someone will _____.

W   All right. Thank you so much and _____.

07 購物／休假

PART 3

STEP 1 題型演練

Ⓐ 先看過題目，再聆聽對話，並選出正確答案。🎧163

M Good morning. How can I help you?

W Hello. I'd like to file a complaint about my room. It smells terrible, and I don't think I can sleep in there another night.

M Oh, I'm so sorry to hear that. Let me see if I can find another room for you. Hmm . . . unfortunately, it looks like we are fully booked. But if you can wait until tomorrow, I can offer you a room upgrade.

W That sounds fine. Please let me know as soon as I can move into the new room.

男 早安。有什麼我能幫您的嗎？

女 您好，我想投訴我房間的問題。裡頭味道很可怕，我覺得我沒辦法在裡面多睡一晚。

男 喔，聽到您這麼說我很抱歉，我查查看能不能為您找到另一間房間。嗯……很遺憾，我們飯店房間全都被訂滿了。但如果您能等到明天，我可以幫您升等。

女 聽起來不錯，那當我能換房間時，麻煩盡快通知我。

Q Why can the woman not change rooms today?

(A) There are no empty rooms.
(B) It is against company policy.
(C) She can't afford a different room.
(D) Her room smells bad.

Q. 為什麼女子今天不能更換房間？

(A) 沒有空房。
(B) 這麼做有違公司政策。
(C) 她負擔不起另一間房間的費用。
(D) 她房間氣味很難聞。

答案 (A)

▶ 本題詢問女子無法更換房間的「原因」。女子要求更換房間，而後男子回答「we are fully booked」（房間全都被訂滿了），等同於沒有空房的意思，因此答案應選 (A)。「fully booked」可替換成「no empty rooms」。

📖 解題重點

- 與購物相關的對話情境，會出現購買商品、換貨、退款等內容。
- 與休假相關的對話情境，會出現預訂、取消機票或飯店等內容。當中經常出現針對商品、飯店服務不滿的客訴。

Ⓑ 再聽一遍上面的對話，並針對題目選出適當的答案。🎧164

1 What is the woman's problem?
(A) The condition of her room is not good.
(B) Her room is too noisy.
(C) There is not enough space in her room.

2 Who most likely is the man?
(A) A sales clerk
(B) A hotel employee
(C) A sales representative

Ⓐ 聆聽下列單字及片語，並跟著唸唸看。 🎧165

❶ 購物相關用語

make a purchase 採購、購買
return an item 退貨
offer a discount 提供折扣
get a discount 享受折扣
overcharge（向某人）索價過高、多收（某人）錢
out of stock 沒有庫存
brand new 全新的、嶄新的
up to 50% 最多達 50%
get a refund 取得退款
free of charge 免付費
exchange A for B 用 A 交換 B
shop for 選購、逛街買……
speak with a manager 和經理談
sold out 賣完了、售罄
on sale 特賣、特價中
additional discount 額外折扣

❷ 休假相關用語

file a complaint 投訴
make a reservation 預約、預訂
confirm a reservation 確認預約
cancel a flight 取消班機
take some time off 休息一下
travel agency 旅行社
itinerary 行程
sightseeing 觀光
go on a cruise 搭郵輪
go on vacation 去度假
go on a trip 去旅遊
travel agent 旅行社職員

Ⓑ 聆聽下面的句子，並完成填空。 🎧166

1 We are _____ when you _____ .
您若在線上購買，我們將提供 10% 的折扣。

2 If you want to _____ , you should _____ .
您如果想退貨，則必須攜帶收據正本。

3 I think I _____ the coat I purchased at your store.
我覺得我在您店裡買外套時被多收錢了。

4 I would like to _____ about the service.
我想和經理談談這項服務。

5 If you purchase 3 items on this shelf, you can _____ .
若您購買三項這個架子上的商品，將能得到額外的折扣。

6 According to this _____ , I am supposed to _____ on the last day.
按照這份行程，我最後一天應該會去觀光。

STEP 3　聽寫練習

A 聆聽對話後，針對題目選出適當的答案。 🎧167

1 What does the man recommend the woman do?

(A) Use a coupon to buy a sale item

(B) Buy several pairs of jeans

(C) Keep her coupon to use at a later date

(D) Browse the new products on sale

> 字彙 **still going on** 還在進行中
> **buy-one-get-one-free deal**
> 買一送一方案
> **as well** 也　**combine** 合併、搭配
> **promotion** 促銷
> **take a look around** 逛逛　**browse** 隨意看

2 What is the problem?

(A) An item is sold out.

(B) The man did not bring his credit card.

(C) A product is broken.

(D) The woman does not have any cash.

> 字彙 **return an item** 退貨　**purchase** 購買
> **give . . . a refund** 給予（某人）退款
> **sold out** 賣完了

B 再聽一遍對話內容，並完成句子填空。 🎧168

1

W Hello. Is your Memorial Day Sale _____?

M It certainly is. _____ are _____, and we have a buy-one-get-one-free deal on any pair of jeans.

W Oh, great. I have a coupon that I _____. Can I use it _____ _____ as well?

M Unfortunately, sale prices _____ any other coupons or _____. I'm sorry about that, but you can _____ and use it _____.

W Okay, well, I think I'll just _____ for now. Thank you.

2

M Hello. I'd like to _____, please.

W All right, sir, I can certainly _____. Do you have the _____ that _____?

M Oh, no, _____ right now, but I have the receipt. Can you _____ _____?

W Unfortunately, we have _____. You will have to return with the card before I can give you a _____.

M I see. Well, I'll have to _____ then. Thank you anyway.

119

實戰演練 Practice Test

A 聆聽下面的對話，並選出正確答案。 169

1 Where most likely does the woman work?

(A) At a hotel
(B) At an airport
(C) At a taxi company
(D) At a restaurant

2 What problem does the man mention?

(A) He lost his wallet.
(B) He wants to make a room reservation.
(C) He would like to speak with the manager.
(D) He forgot his reservation number.

3 What most likely will the woman do next?

(A) Send the man his wallet
(B) Close the reception desk
(C) Call her manager
(D) Reserve a room for the man

4 What is the man shopping for?

(A) Art supplies
(B) An oven
(C) Flowers
(D) Flour

5 What does Leeroy say about the item?

(A) The store is sold out of it.
(B) It is sold at a different branch of the store.
(C) He sold the last of the stock this morning.
(D) It is on sale for a reduced price.

6 What most likely will the customer do next?

(A) Place an order for a product
(B) Negotiate the price of an item
(C) Go to another store location
(D) Ask to speak with the manager

B 再聽一遍對話內容，並完成句子填空。 🎧 170

[1-3]

M   Hello. _____ because I stayed there last night, and I think _____

_____ in the room when I _____.

W   You did? Okay, let me _____. What room were you staying in?

M   Room 505. I was there _____ and checked out this morning.

W   Yes, it seems that a member of the staff gave your wallet _____

_____ here. _____ and pick it up _____

_____ for you.

M   Oh, no. _____, so there is no way _____.

Can you have it _____?

W   You'll have to _____ about that. _____.

[4-6]

W   Good morning. How may I help you?

M1   Hi. _____ whole wheat flour? I'd like to _____

for my bakery.

W   Whole wheat flour? I think we do, but _____. Hey, Leeroy, _____

_____ whole wheat flour?

M2   Yeah, but _____. You have to _____

for that. Or we can order it and _____.

M1   Okay, _____ I'll just _____. Thanks so

much for the help.

08 交通／公共場所

Ⓐ 先看過題目，再聆聽對話，並選出正確答案。🎧171

M	I'm sorry, but could you tell me where I can get the train to Buffalo? I'm not sure which platform I need to go to.
W	Of course. Are you taking the local train or the express train?
M	It doesn't really matter, so I'll take whichever is departing sooner.
W	That would be the local train. You can get the train at platform 8. Make sure you keep your ticket on you at all times.
M	Great. Thank you so much for your help.

男	不好意思，您能告訴我去水牛城要去哪裡搭火車嗎？我不確定要去哪個月台才對。
女	當然好。您要搭普通車還是特快車呢？
男	都可以，我想要愈早出發愈好。
女	這樣的話請搭普通車，您可以到 8 號月台搭乘。請您記得隨時把票準備好。
男	太好了，非常感謝您的幫忙。

Q What does the man mean when he says, "It doesn't really matter"?

(A) He does not know the difference.

(B) He does not mind which train he takes.

(C) He does not agree with the woman.

(D) He cannot decide yet.

Q. 男子說「都可以」，意思為何？

(A) 他不知道有何差別。

(B) 搭哪種車他都不介意。

(C) 他不同意女子的說法。

(D) 他還沒辦法決定。

答案 (B)

▶ 題目引用對話中的句子時，請務必確認清楚該句話前後方出現的內容。男子表示「It doesn't really matter」（都可以），因而必須確認該句話之前的狀況。而前面女子詢問男子要搭乘普通車還是特快車，因此答案要選 (B)。

📖 解題重點

- 與交通或公共場所有關，指的是對話發生在火車站、圖書館、醫院、電影院、不動產、郵局等地方。
- 若能整理出與各地點相關的對話情境、單字和用法，將有助於理解整篇對話的內容。

Ⓑ 再聽一遍上面的對話，並針對題目選出適當的答案。🎧172

1 What train will the man probably take to Buffalo?

(A) An express train

(B) A subway train

(C) A local train

2 What will the man do next?

(A) Check a train schedule

(B) Buy a train ticket

(C) Go to a platform

STEP 2 常考用法

Ⓐ 聆聽下列單字及片語，並跟著唸唸看。🎧173

❶ 交通方式、交通狀況相關用語

catch a train 趕上火車
miss a bus 錯過公車
get on/off a bus 上／下公車
board a subway 搭乘地鐵
detour 繞道
traffic jam/congestion 塞車、交通堵塞
get stuck in traffic 塞車、卡在車陣中
transfer 轉乘
platform 月台
ticket office 售票處
intersection 十字路口
crosswalk 行人穿越道
one-way ticket 單程票
round-trip ticket 來回票
road sign 交通號誌
car crash 車禍、撞車
parking lot 停車場
pedestrian 行人
traffic light 紅綠燈
get a flat tire 爆胎

❷ 醫院、電影院相關用語

medical checkup 健康檢查
have an appointment 有門診預約
fill out a document 填寫文件
insurance coverage 承保範圍
symptom 症狀
reception 接待處
medication 藥物治療
action/horror film 動作片／恐怖片
sci-fi movie 科幻電影
plot 情節
cast 卡司、演員陣容

❸ 圖書館、不動產相關用語

return a book 還書
check out a book 借（出）書
additional charge 額外費用
real estate office 不動產業者
realtor 房地產仲介
property 房產、地產、建築
rent an apartment 租公寓
pay one's rent 付房租

Ⓑ 聆聽下面的句子，並完成填空。🎧174

1 If you are over forty years old, you _____ on a regular basis.

您如果超過四十歲，便應該定期做健康檢查。

2 There are _____ at this time of day.

每天這時候的行人很多。

3 Mr. Yamamoto _____ on his way to work.

山本先生在上班途中塞車了。

4 You are allowed to _____ at a time.

您一次可借五本書。

5 We had better leave now _____ to Boston.

為了趕上 11 點開往波士頓的火車，我們最好現在就出發。

6 A headache and a stomachache are _____ of the flu.

頭痛和胃痛是流感最常見的症狀。

A 聆聽對話後，針對題目選出適當的答案。 🎧 175

1 What will the man most likely do next?

(A) Go to a train station

(B) Take an elevator

(C) Buy a ticket to Madrid

(D) Wait for a bus at a platform

TIME	DOCTOR
12:30-1:30	Dr. Kelly
2:00-3:00	Dr. Lee
3:30-4:30	Dr. Palmer
5:00-6:00	Dr. Yang

2 Look at the graphic. Who will the man meet for an X-ray?

(A) Dr. Kelly   (C) Dr. Palmer

(B) Dr. Lee   (D) Dr. Yang

字彙 **transfer** 轉乘 **get to** 到達（某地）
destination 目的地

字彙 **appointment** 門診預約
fill out 填寫（表格等） **insurance** 保險

B 再聽一遍對話內容，並完成句子填空。 🎧 176

1

M Excuse me. Can I use this ticket to _____? I'm _____ _____ Madrid.

W Let's see. I'm sorry, but bus tickets can _____ if your ticket is _____. You bought your ticket _____ _____, so you _____ to get to your destination.

M Oh, I see. Do you know _____?

W It's just right there _____.

2

M Hello. My name is Keith Little. I _____ for an X-ray at 2:30 P.M. today.

W All right, I see _____ to visit our office. Here, please _____ while you wait. A nurse will call you when _____.

M Great. Do you need _____? I have it right here.

W Oh, yes, thank you. I'll _____.

A 聆聽下面的對話，並選出正確答案。🎧 177

1 Where most likely are the speakers?

(A) At a movie theater

(B) At a shopping mall

(C) At a bookstore

(D) At a library

2 What does the man suggest the woman do?

(A) Pay a fine today

(B) Purchase a book

(C) Come back another time

(D) Bring some more books

3 What does the man mostly likely mean when he says, "I'm afraid not"?

(A) He will cancel a fine.

(B) The woman cannot use a credit card.

(C) Late fees are expensive.

(D) There is not an ATM nearby.

TITLE	TIME	PRICE
The Last Battle	10 A.M.	$6.00
	11 A.M.	$7.00
	3 P.M.	$8.00
	7 P.M.	$9.00

4 Why is the man calling?

(A) To ask for directions

(B) To ask the woman to go out

(C) To cancel a reservation

(D) To ask about a cost

5 Look at the graphic. How much will the speakers pay for each ticket?

(A) $6.00

(B) $7.00

(C) $8.00

(D) $9.00

6 What does the man say about the restaurant?

(A) It opened recently.

(B) It is close to the theater.

(C) It is being renovated.

(D) It has a bad reputation.

B 再聽一遍對話內容，並完成句子填空。 🎧 178

[1-3]

W   Hello. _____ these books, please. Here is _____ .

M   All right, let's take a look. Oh, it seems that _____
_____ by a week. You'll have to _____ .

W   Oh, really? I didn't realize that it was late. Hmm . . . _____
_____ on me. Is it possible to _____ ?

M   I'm afraid not. But there is _____ that you can use. I
_____ today to _____ .

[4-6]

M   Hello, Rachel. I'm _____ tomorrow. Do you want to
go with me?

W   Sure, _____ . What do you _____ ?

M   Well, I want to see the new action film *The Last Battle*, but I'm not sure
_____ . What do you think?

W   Hmm . . . Let's see a morning show _____ . How
about _____ ?

M   Good idea. We _____ , too. I know a good
restaurant _____ .

A 選出正確的中文意思。

1　take inventory　　　　(A) 盤點存貨　　(B) 陳列商品

2　business premises　　(A) 商業建築　　(B) 商業設備

3　state-of-the-art　　　 (A) 先進的　　　(B) 過時的

4　make a complaint　　 (A) 投訴　　　　(B) 讚賞

5　document envelope　　(A) 公文配送　　(B) 公文封

B 圈選出與中文意思相符的單字。

1　我想問您店裡有沒有賣最新型的筆電。

　➡ I wonder if you (hold / carry) the latest laptops in the store.

2　對於這可能造成的不便，我們深感抱歉。

　➡ We are really sorry for the (indifference / inconvenience) this might cause.

3　因為時間緊迫，我認為你應該用快遞寄這份合約。

　➡ I think you should send the contract by express service since it is (overdue / urgent).

4　史密斯先生將在會議室安裝攜帶式投影機。

　➡ Mr. Smith will (set up / check out) the portable projector in the meeting room.

5　按照這份行程，我們最後一天會去羅馬。

　➡ According to this (minute / itinerary), we are going to Rome on the last day.

C 將括號內的單字按正確的順序排列組合成句子。

1　Ms. Tailor _____ on the way here. (in / got / traffic / stuck)
　泰勒女士在來這裡的路上塞車了。

2　All of our winter clothing lines _____. (to / are / 50% / up / off)
　我們全系列冬裝商品最高可享五折。

3　The construction _____ tomorrow.
　(until / supposed / isn't / to / start)
　工程應該明天才開始。

4　The doctor advised me to _____.
　(get / a regular / on / a medical checkup / basis)
　醫生建議我定期做健康檢查。

5　Please step over to the counter and _____.
　(fill / this / out / form)
　請到櫃檯填寫這份表格。

PART 4

簡短獨白
Short Talks

STEP 1 題型演練

Ⓐ 先看題目，再聆聽獨白，並選出正確答案。🎧179

M The end of the semester is here, and you know what that means: it's time to sell back your used textbooks. Here at Barney's Books, we offer the best prices to students selling their books. In fact, if the university bookstore offers a better price, we guarantee that we will match its price. Mention this ad at any of our locations, and you can receive a free bookbag when selling your used books to us.	男 學期末到了，你懂意思吧：該賣二手教科書囉。我們巴尼書屋給學生的賣書價格是最優惠的。說真的，如果大學書店價格更好，我們保證給你同樣的價格。你在我們的任何門市賣二手書時，別忘了跟我們說你看過這則廣告，你將獲贈一個免費的書包。
Q What can customers receive if they mention the advertisement? (A) A discount (B) A free gift (C) An extended warranty (D) A coupon book	Q. 顧客如果提到這則廣告，可以獲得什麼？ (A) 折扣 (B) 免費贈品 (C) 延長保固 (D) 一本優惠券 答案 (B)

▶ 本題詢問看過該廣告的顧客可以獲得什麼東西。後半段廣告文中提到「跟店員說你看過這則廣告，你將獲贈一個免費的書包」（Mention this ad at any of our locations, and you can receive a free bookbag），因此答案為 (B)。選項將文中的「free bookbag」改寫為「free gift」。

解題重點

- 與廣告相關的獨白，會出現產品、服務、新設施、活動等相關內容。
- 廣告題型中經常出現詢問相關細節的考題，因此請務必先看過題目，快速掌握題目重點，以便在聆聽獨白時找出所需的資訊。

Ⓑ 再聽一遍上面的獨白，並針對題目選出適當的答案。🎧180

1 What is being advertised?

(A) An opportunity to sell used books

(B) An opportunity to buy used books

(C) A university bookstore

2 Why does the man say, "we guarantee that we will match its price"?

(A) To show that a store provides the best books

(B) To explain why the prices are so high

(C) To show that a store offers the best prices

STEP 2 常考用法

A 聆聽下列單字及片語，並跟著唸唸看。 🎧181

1 產品廣告相關用語

a wide range of 有很多種類的……
a new line 新系列產品
fit the needs 滿足需求
durable 耐用的、持久的
get up to 50% 最多達50%
feature 以……為特色、標榜
special offer 特別優惠
voucher 兌換券
clearance sale 出清特賣、清倉大拍賣
buy one, get one free 買一送一
for a limited time 限時、在有限時間內
extended warranty 延長保固
only last until 只持續到……
request a free sample 索取免費試用品

2 設施、活動廣告相關用語

grand opening 盛大開幕（式）
recently renovated 最近整修好的
located in the heart of 位處……的中心
celebrate a special occasion 慶祝特別的事
enter a contest 參賽
for further information 欲知詳情
better facilities 更好的設施
trial period 試用期
biggest sale of the year 年度最大檔特賣
spacious rooms 寬敞的房間／會議室
accommodate 容納
stop by 短暫光顧、順路造訪
sign up for 報名參加
find out more 進一步了解

B 聆聽下面的句子，並完成填空。 🎧182

1 We are offering special promotions in order to _____.
為了慶祝盛大開幕，我們正在舉行特別促銷。

2 Please visit our website or _____ one of our stores to _____.
想進一步了解這筆交易內容，請上我們的官網或光臨我們的店面。

3 The special offer will _____ this Friday.
特別優惠活動只到這週五。

4 Our new store is _____ downtown.
我們的新店面位於市中心的核心地帶，交通便利。

5 If you would like to _____, please _____ and contact information on the list.
您如果有意參賽，請在名單上寫下名字和聯絡方式。

6 The new _____ provides _____ and can _____ more than a thousand people.
新會議中心擁有寬敞的會議室，可容納一千人以上。

STEP 3 聽寫練習

A 聆聽獨白後，針對題目選出適當的答案。 🎧 183

1 What service is being advertised?

    (A) A mobile phone service

    (B) An advertisement service

    (C) An Internet provider service

    (D) A computer repair service

> 字彙 **offer** 提供　**fit the needs** 滿足需求
> **Internet provider** 網路供應商

2 What does the speaker emphasize about the app?

    (A) It is simple and easy to use.

    (B) It is very inexpensive.

    (C) It comes with great customer service.

    (D) It is very modern.

> 字彙 **foreign language** 外語
> **be satisfied with** 對⋯⋯感到滿意
> **app** 應用程式　**vocabulary** 單字（量）
> **convenient** 方便的　**sign up** 註冊

B 再聽一遍獨白內容，並完成句子填空。 🎧 184

1

M _____ slow download speeds. That's why Next Edge Internet _____ the fastest Internet speeds possible to our city. We _____ that will _____. _____ for details on our home and business Internet plans. Next Edge: it doesn't get any faster.

2

W Do you spend hours and hours _____ but aren't _____? Well, then Word Wise is just the app for you! We understand _____ to learn a new language, so that's why we have developed an easy way _____ every day right _____ anytime and anywhere! It is _____ to improve your vocabulary. _____ is fast and easy, so download Word Wise today!

A 聆聽下面的獨白，並選出正確答案。 185

1 What business is being advertised?

(A) A medical clinic

(B) A mechanic's shop

(C) A gym

(D) A golf course

Percy's Department Coupon

Expires 06/15

Additional 10% off

Limit one coupon per person
Can be combined with offline promotions

---

2 What can customers receive for free?

(A) A membership

(B) Transportation

(C) Training equipment

(D) Personal training

4 What is being advertised?

(A) A new service

(B) A new product

(C) A relocation

(D) A sale

3 Which type of membership can customers receive a special discount on?

(A) 1-month

(B) 3-month

(C) 6-month

(D) 12-month

5 What does the speaker say will happen on Monday?

(A) A new store will open.

(B) A product will be released.

(C) A sale will end.

(D) An event will begin.

6 Look at the graphic. At which location can the coupon be used?

(A) Manoa

(B) Pikoi

(C) Windward

(D) All Percy stores

[1-3]

M Are you looking for a way to _____ this year? Here at Flying
Jay Fitness, we can help! Our gyms have the _____
every kind of exercise routine. _____, we also
provide one month of _____ to help you _____.
And _____, we are _____ yearly
memberships! Start the new year right with Flying Jay Fitness!

[4-6]

W In order to celebrate the grand opening of the Manoa location, Percy's
Department Store is having _____! You can
_____ products, _____ fashion, cosmetics,
and outdoor gear, at all of our stores. _____ is that
we are offering coupons for an additional 10% discount only at the newly
opened store. Other stores, such as those in Pikoi and Windward, offer only
30% discounts. _____. And don't forget
to _____ that will help you _____!

02 廣播

STEP 1 題型演練

A 先看題目，再聆聽獨白，並選出正確答案。 187

W And now for some local news. Highway 14 between Denver and Culver City will be closed until the end of September because of a major construction project. City planners say that the highway must be closed to expand the number of lanes to eight. Drivers should use Highway 36 to travel between the two cities during this time. Stay tuned for international news coming up next.

女 現在請收聽地方新聞。因為大型建設計畫的關係，丹佛和卡爾弗城之間的 14 號公路到 9 月底前都將封閉。都市計畫人員表示這條公路必須封閉，才能拓寬成八線道。這段期間，駕駛朋友必須使用 36 號公路來往這兩座城市。不要轉台，請繼續收聽接下來的國際新聞。

Q According to the report, what will happen until September?

(A) A road will be closed.

(B) A building will be constructed.

(C) A new railway will be built.

(D) Tourists will receive free bus passes.

Q. 根據報導，到 9 月之前會如何？

(A) 一條道路將封閉。

(B) 一棟建築物將蓋好。

(C) 一條新鐵路將建好。

(D) 遊客將獲得免費公車通行證。

答案 (A)

▶ 新聞廣播節目中提到 14 號高速公路將封閉至 9 月底，因此答案為 (A) A road will be closed（一條道路將封閉）。

💡 解題重點

• 廣播題型中，出題頻率較高的主題有天氣預報、交通路況、區域新聞、商業新聞、娛樂新聞等，建議整理出各大主題的常考單字和用法。

B 再聽一遍上面的獨白，並針對題目選出適當的答案。 188

1 What are the listeners advised to do?

(A) Stay indoors

(B) Use public transportation

(C) Take an alternative route

2 What will the listeners hear next?

(A) An interview

(B) Business news

(C) International news

Ⓐ 聆聽下列單字及片語，並跟著唸唸看。 🎧189

❶ 一般新聞相關用語

stay tuned 不要轉台、繼續收聽
tune in to 轉台到……
listen to 收聽……
host 主持人
local news 地方新聞
correspondent 通訊記者、特派員
be back in an hour 一小時後回來
be scheduled for 安排給……
business update 最新商業報導
commercial break 廣告休息時間

❷ 交通相關用語

commuter 通勤族
on the way to work 上班途中
public transportation 大眾運輸
traffic report 路況資訊
traffic update 路況資訊更新
highway 公路、幹道
alternative route 替代道路
under construction 興建中、施工中
be backed up 堵車

❸ 天氣相關用語

weather forecast 氣象預報
latest weather report 最新氣象報導
temperature 溫度、氣溫
drop dramatically（氣溫）急遽下降
slippery 滑的、易滑的
heat wave 熱浪
fog/hail/shower 霧／冰雹／陣雨
snowstorm 暴風雪
thunderstorm 大雷雨
humid 潮濕的

❹ 運動、採訪相關用語

thank you for joining 感謝您一起收聽……
tournament 錦標賽
stadium 體育場
release an album 出專輯
interview the mayor 訪問市長
entertainment 娛樂
renowned 著名的
award-winning 獲獎肯定的
ask listeners to call in 邀請聽眾來電

Ⓑ 聆聽下面的句子，並完成填空。 🎧190

1 We'll be back _____ , so _____ for the latest business news.

廣告之後馬上回來，請接著收聽最新商業新聞。

2 You're advised to _____ due to _____ on Highway 87.

由於 87 號公路拓寬工程的關係，建議您利用大眾運輸。

3 We _____ about the new road _____ .

我們將訪問市長有關新的道路建設計畫一事。

4 It will _____ and _____ this week.

這週將持續極端的濕熱天氣。

5 _____ are very frustrated because Highway 14 _____ .

14 號公路將在 8 月封閉，讓通勤族感到十分無奈。

6 The temperature _____ in the evening.

氣溫預計今晚就會急遽下降。

STEP 3　聽寫練習

A 聆聽獨白後，針對題目選出適當的答案。 🎧191

1 What are listeners encouraged to do?

(A) Call in with questions

(B) Open small businesses

(C) Attend an open meeting

(D) Try to save more money

2 What does the speaker imply when she says, "Tickets are going fast"?

(A) There is a discount on tickets.

(B) Tickets are not required to see the show.

(C) A show is very popular.

(D) An artist received good reviews.

> 字彙 **special guest** 特別來賓
> **financial crisis** 金融危機　**affect** 影響
> **handle** 處理

> 字彙 **fair** 市集　**ride** 遊樂設施
> **feature** 以……為特色、標榜

B 再聽一遍獨白內容，並完成句子填空。 🎧192

1　**M**　Good morning and ＿＿＿＿＿＿＿＿＿＿ KKL Radio. Today, we ＿＿＿＿＿＿
＿＿＿＿＿＿＿＿＿＿, Dr. Alicia Gonzalez, a professor of economics and
finance at the University of Colorado. For the next hour, Dr. Gonzalez is going
to help us understand ＿＿＿＿＿＿＿＿＿＿ small
businesses in the area. She will also share some advice on ＿＿＿＿＿＿
＿＿＿＿＿＿ better. At the end of the show, we ＿＿＿＿＿＿＿＿＿ for
Dr. Gonzalez to answer your questions, so I ＿＿＿＿＿＿＿＿＿ at
that time.

2　**W**　＿＿＿＿＿＿＿＿＿＿＿＿ Radio MBB. Don't forget that the Douglas
County Fair will be ＿＿＿＿＿＿＿＿＿＿, October 21. You can enjoy
the fair rides, the games, and, of course, the fair food! On Saturday, there
will be a giant pumpkin competition. You can find out who grew the biggest
pumpkin. It will be great fun for all the family, and you can get free pumpkin
seeds. On Sunday, the fair will feature a special musical artist, the Jason
Byer Band! ＿＿＿＿＿＿＿＿＿＿＿＿, so check out the county fair
website ＿＿＿＿＿＿＿＿＿.

A 聆聽下面的獨白，並選出正確答案。 🎧 193

1 What is the report mainly about?

(A) A canceled game

(B) A new player joining a team

(C) A new stadium opening

(D) An important game taking place

2 Why does the speaker say, "you should get there early"?

(A) The weather will not be good.

(B) There are a limited number of free gifts.

(C) Parking will be restricted.

(D) Tickets will be sold out.

3 According to the report, what will happen if the team hits a homerun?

(A) A team will win a trophy.

(B) A visitor can keep the ball.

(C) A restaurant will give away free food.

(D) The game will end.

4 What does the speaker say will happen this week?

(A) It will continue to rain.

(B) An event will be canceled because of the weather.

(C) There will be a snowstorm.

(D) A building will be built.

5 What does the speaker mean when she says, "It is not a surprise during hurricane season"?

(A) No one can predict hurricanes.

(B) This weather is typical during this time.

(C) The rain will stop.

(D) It will be very windy.

6 When does the speaker suggest going outside?

(A) On Tuesday

(B) On Wednesday

(C) On Friday

(D) On Sunday

B 再聽一遍獨白內容，並完成句子填空。 🎧194

[1-3]

M _____ on WTZ Radio _____ .
Tomorrow is finally the big game between our own Wildcats and _____
_____ , the Bears. This is the last game of the season,
so there will be _____ at the game. _____
_____ to arrive at the baseball stadium will receive a free Wildcats
baseball cap, so you _____ . In addition, if the
Wildcats _____ , Tony's Tacos will _____
per customer after the game! If you _____ live, you
can always _____ on the local TV channel.

[4-6]

W And now for _____ . Overall, _____ ,
but it looks like we will be _____ this week. _____
_____ during hurricane season here in Louisiana. But
don't get too depressed. Fortunately, _____ this coming
Friday, so I suggest you take this chance to _____ .
It would be a great time to _____ on 5th Avenue.

03 電話留言

STEP 1 題型演練

A 先看題目，再聆聽獨白，並選出正確答案。 195

M Hi, Igor. This is Steven Weber from Downtown Realty. I have some exciting news. I showed a couple your house for sale, and they made an offer to buy it! I think that you will be happy with the offer that they made, but I want to meet you in person to discuss it. I will be out of town from Wednesday through Sunday, so I would like to meet you before I leave if possible. Let me know when you are available, and we can make some plans.	男 伊格爾您好，我是下城房地產的史蒂芬・韋伯，我有些令人雀躍的好消息要告訴您。您想出售的房子我給一對夫婦看過了，他們出價想買。我猜您會滿意他們開的價格，但我想當面和您討論一下。我週三到週日不在鎮上，如果可以的話，我想在趁我還在時和您見一面。請讓我知道您何時有空，我們可以安排一下見面。

Q Where does the man most likely work?

(A) At a museum

(B) At a real estate agency

(C) At an IT company

(D) At a moving company

Q. 男子最有可能在哪裡工作？

(A) 博物館

(B) 房屋仲介公司

(C) 資訊科技公司

(D) 搬家公司

答案 (B)

▶ 男子於留言開頭處介紹自己是任職於 Downtown Realty（下城房地產）的 Steven Weber（史蒂芬・韋伯），由此可知男子在房屋仲介公司（real estate agency）工作。雖然 realty 的意思為「房地產」，但在獨白中指的是公司名稱，由此可以推測該單字在獨白中的意思為「房屋仲介公司」。

解題重點

- 電話留言題型中，會出現來電者留下語音留言或是自動語音錄音等內容。
- 該類題型的題目經常會詢問留下語音留言的目的、留言者的職業，或其他相關細節。

B 再聽一遍上面的獨白，並針對題目選出適當的答案。 196

1 What news does the man deliver to the listener?

(A) Somebody wants to buy his house.

(B) Somebody wants to sell a house to him.

(C) A couple wants to meet him in person.

2 What does the speaker ask the listener to do?

(A) Make an offer

(B) Contact him

(C) Leave the town

STEP 2 常考用法

A 聆聽下列單字、片語及句型,並跟著唸唸看。 197

1 表明來電目的

I am calling about . . .
我打電話來,是為了說有關……的事
I am responding to . . .
針對……,我現在答覆
I have some news 我有些消息
I have an inquiry about . . .
對於……我有個疑問

2 表明無法接聽的理由

be out of town 不在鎮上
not available
(人)沒空的 、(物)不可用的 、(物)不可取得的
be away 不在、離開
I am currently attending . . .
我目前正在參加……

3 自我介紹、表明任職公司

Hello. This is . . . 哈囉,我是(誰)
Hi. It is . . . 嗨,我是(誰)
I am calling from . . .
這是來自(哪裡、公司等)的電話
This is . . . from . . .
這是(誰)從(哪裡、公司等)打的電話

4 留言結束前

call me back 回電給我
You can reach me at . . .
您可以撥打(電話號碼)聯絡到我
feel free to contact me 儘管聯絡我
Don't hesitate to . . .(別客氣)儘管做(某事)

B 聆聽下面的句子,並完成填空。 198

1 _____ the order you placed on our website.

我打這通電話給您,是有關於您在我們網站所下的訂單一事。

2 _____ the room I made a reservation for the other day.

我對於幾天前預約的房間有個疑問。

3 _____ for 2 weeks starting this Friday, so if you have any questions, you can email me.

我從這週五開始兩週不在鎮上,所以如果您有任何問題,都可以寫電子郵件給我。

4 _____ my office number, 555-2424, during office hours.

上班時間您可以撥打我的辦公室電話 555-2424 聯絡到我。

5 _____ at my cell phone number if you have any further inquiries.

如果您還有任何疑問,儘管撥打我的手機號碼跟我聯絡。

6 I _____ you made about the cleaning service.

您曾提出清潔服務的需求,我現在給您答覆。

A 聆聽獨白後，針對題目選出適當的答案。🎧199

1 What problem does the woman mention?

(A) Some customer details are incorrect.

(B) An event was canceled.

(C) An item is sold out.

(D) A payment is overdue.

> 字彙 monthly 每月的 phone bill 電話帳單
> charge 收費 late fee 逾期罰款
> submit 繳交 payment 付款金額
> sold out 賣光了 overdue 逾期

2 What does the speaker want to do?

(A) Verify personal information

(B) Close an account

(C) Place an order

(D) Request a refund

> 字彙 sign up for 註冊 account 帳戶
> misspell 拼錯
> call . . . back 回電（給某人）
> verify 確認
> personal information 個人資訊
> place an order 下訂單 refund 退款

B 再聽一遍獨白內容，並完成句子填空。🎧200

1

W Hello. _____ Lakeshore Telecommunications _____. It seems that you still haven't _____, so we have to _____. _____, because your payment is _____, the charge will be _____. Please pay _____ as soon as possible. As always, you can _____, by mail, or online. If you have any questions, don't _____ anytime. Thank you.

2

M Hello. This is Feliciano Manetto, and _____ I am having _____ with your website. I am trying to _____, but I _____ _____. It says that the customer information doesn't _____ _____. However, I _____ last week, so I am sure nothing has changed. I think maybe my name is _____ _____. Could you _____ and _____ how you have my name _____? Thanks.

Ⓐ 聆聽下面的獨白，並選出正確答案。 201

Quarter 1	Sales Totals by Department
Men's Apparel	*$2,450.00*
Women's Apparel	*$420,000.00*
Shoes	*$9,500.00*
Accessories	*$8,900.00*

1 What is the purpose of the message?

(A) To ask about an error
(B) To set up a meeting
(C) To confirm a purchase
(D) To apply for a position

2 What does the speaker ask the listener to do?

(A) Increase sales
(B) Contact customers
(C) Reexamine some information
(D) Order an item

3 Look at the graphic. What department does the speaker ask about?

(A) Men's Apparel
(B) Women's Apparel
(C) Shoes
(D) Accessories

4 Why is an event being held?

(A) To commemorate a holiday
(B) To promote a product
(C) To celebrate a retirement
(D) To encourage teamwork

5 What does the speaker say about the Italian restaurant?

(A) It is very delicious.
(B) It has a convenient location.
(C) It doesn't have an appropriate menu.
(D) It is not available for an event.

6 What does the speaker imply when he says, "Who knows if we can find one in time"?

(A) He does not understand the industry.
(B) He is not sure if he can find a caterer before an event.
(C) He wants to ask someone else for help with a party.
(D) He needs to call a restaurant again.

143

B 再聽一遍獨白內容，並完成句子填空。 🎧 202

[1-3]

M   Hello. It's Alexander. I was _____ that you sent me earlier this week, but something _____. One of the _____ from the first quarter _____. Are you sure _____? I mean, it's way higher than any of the other items, so I think you _____ too many zeros. Anyway, _____ and _____ when you can. Thanks.

[4-6]

M   Hi. It's Peter. _____ the Christmas office party _____ _____ next week. I called the Italian restaurant that _____ _____, but they said that they're _____ of our party. We _____ as soon as possible. Do you know _____ that can _____? Who knows if we can find one in time? Anyway, _____, and _____ _____ together. Thanks.

04 會議／公告

STEP 1 題型演練

A 先看題目，再聆聽獨白，並選出正確答案。🎧 203

W Good afternoon and thank you for joining this meeting today. I'd like to discuss a change that will affect all tellers at our bank. From now on, you have to sign in to your workstation by using a personal ID code. The goal is to help us track our customer interactions better. The bank system will remain the same, so don't worry about that. Just check your email, and you'll find your new individual log-in ID.

女 午安，感謝大家來參加今天這場會議。我想討論一項異動，這項異動將會影響到我們銀行的全體櫃員。從現在開始，你們需要用個人身分代碼登入你們的工作站，這麼做的目標是要幫助我們把客戶互動追蹤做得更好。銀行系統將維持原狀，所以不用太擔心。請大家記得確認一下電子信箱，你們會看到你們新的個人登錄帳號。

Q Who most likely are the listeners?

(A) Nurses

(B) Tellers

(C) Cashiers

(D) Receptionists

Q. 聽眾最有可能是誰？

(A) 護士

(B) 櫃員

(C) 收銀員

(D) 接待人員

答案 (B)

▶ 獨白中表示要談論的內容為與所有銀行櫃員有關的異動（I'd like to discuss a change that will affect all tellers at our bank），因此答案應選 (B) Tellers（櫃員）。

🔒 解題重點

● 公司內部會議和公告事項題型中，會出現談論會議中的案子，或告知員工公司內部的變化等內容。而該類題型的題目經常會詢問主旨、目的，以及建議或要求事項。

B 再聽一遍上面的獨白，並針對題目選出適當的答案。🎧 204

1 According to the speaker, what is the reason for the change?

(A) To track interactions better

(B) To evaluate tellers better

(C) To hire more tellers

2 What are the listeners asked to do after the meeting?

(A) Contact customers

(B) Create a new ID code

(C) Check their email

Ⓐ 聆聽下列單字、片語及句型，並跟著唸唸看。 🎧 205

1 會議相關用語

discuss the results 討論結果
thank you for joining 感謝你（們）參加
staff meeting 員工大會
call a meeting 召開會議
meeting agenda 會議議程
bring some ideas 提出一些想法
share opinions 分享意見
pass around a copy 把影本傳下去
distribute a handout 分發資料
submit a report 繳交報告
review a policy 檢討政策、審查政策
promote a product 促銷某產品
come up with ideas 想出點子
invest in . . . 在……上投資
have pros and cons 有利有弊、具有優缺點
previous meeting 上次會議
cast a vote 投票

2 公告相關用語

make an announcement 宣布（某事）
be pleased to announce . . . 很高興地宣布……
congratulate the team on . . .
為（某事）恭喜團隊
the goal is to . . . 目標是讓……
as of today 到今日為止
from now on 從現在起
fill out a survey 填問卷
win an award 得獎
make a name 闖出名號
practical changes 實際變動
take place 舉行
new payroll system 新的薪資系統
demonstrate 展示
you'll be asked to . . . 你（們）將被要求……
sign up for 報名參加、註冊、申請
extra cost 額外費用
work closely with . . . 與……密切合作

Ⓑ 聆聽下面的句子，並完成填空。 🎧 206

1 I _____ that we will soon _____ in London.
　 我很高興地宣布，我們即將在倫敦開設新的分公司。

2 I would like you to _____ .
　 我希望你（們）能想出提高銷售量的方案。

3 _____ with one another.
　 這麼做的目標是要幫助員工彼此溝通更有效率。

4 Both of these suppliers _____ .
　 這兩家供應商各有利弊。

5 The CEO is getting _____ tomorrow morning.
　 執行長準備在明天早上宣布一件事。

6 The management is _____ .
　 高層目前正在考慮採用新的薪資系統。

STEP 3 聽寫練習

A 聆聽獨白後，針對題目選出適當的答案。 🎧207

1 What does the speaker say about the design team?

(A) It won an award.

(B) All of its members are new hires.

(C) It saved the company money.

(D) It developed a new system.

字彙 **award** 獎、獎項　**congratulate** 恭喜　**promote** 提升

2 What does the speaker ask the listeners to do?

(A) Discuss advantages and disadvantages

(B) Review documents

(C) Nominate a candidate

(D) Decide between two options

字彙 **process** 過程　**narrow down** 限縮（範圍）

B 再聽一遍獨白內容，並完成句子填空。 🎧208

1

M Before we start today's meeting, _____. Last week, our S-Series Furniture line won the Best Modern Design Award at the International Furniture Awards in Frankfurt, Germany! I'd like to _____ _____. This will really _____ for our company, and it is _____ here. In the future, I would like the design team _____ the marketing team to _____ this furniture line.

2

M Welcome, everybody, to the Youth Support Committee. As you know, we are _____ to invest in for young people in our city. _____, we _____ to two choices: building a new community center and _____. Both options _____, which we have _____. Today, I would like you all _____ between the two.

Ⓐ 聆聽下面的獨白，並選出正確答案。 209

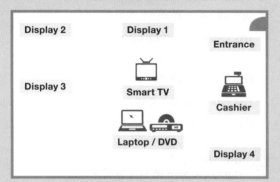

1 Who most likely are the listeners?

(A) Customers
(B) Suppliers
(C) Mechanics
(D) Store staff members

2 How can customers get a discount on TV accessories?

(A) By bringing a coupon
(B) By purchasing a smart TV
(C) By signing up online
(D) By recommending a friend

3 Look at the graphic. Where will the TV accessories be displayed?

(A) Display area 1
(B) Display area 2
(C) Display area 3
(D) Display area 4

4 What problem is the speaker discussing?

(A) A drop in international customers
(B) A problematic employee
(C) A lack of workplace diversity
(D) The need for layoffs

5 What does the speaker ask the listeners to do at the next meeting?

(A) Arrive early
(B) Share their opinions
(C) Submit their sales reports
(D) Review a company policy

6 What will the speaker most likely do next?

(A) Take customer orders
(B) Distribute a handout
(C) Begin a meeting
(D) Hire a new employee

B 再聽一遍獨白內容，並完成句子填空。 🎧 210

[1-3]

W All right, everyone, we _____ for this weekend's big
sale. Now, I think we should move our top-selling TV accessories _____
_____ during the sale so that customers _____.
It's _____ and _____, too, so it
will be easy to introduce them to customers. Remember that _____
_____ can _____ on any TV
accessories they buy. In addition, all laptops and DVD players _____
_____, too. I want to see higher sales of them if possible.

[4-6]

M Okay, one last thing before we _____. I want to talk about
_____. Last year, we had 22%
_____ so far this year. I'm really concerned
about this, and I _____. At
our next meeting, _____ about _____
_____. Here, I'll pass around a copy of the data for you.

A 選出正確的中文意思。

1 extended warranty　　　　　(A) 延長保固　　　　(B) 保固期滿
2 alternative route　　　　　(A) 替代道路　　　　(B) 選擇道路
3 commercial break　　　　　(A) 商業廣告失策　　(B) 商業廣告時間
4 personal information　　　　(A) 人事資訊　　　　(B) 個人資訊
5 extra cost　　　　　　　　(A) 非必要費用　　　(B) 額外費用

B 圈選出與中文意思相符的單字。

1 為了慶祝盛大開幕，我們店今年最大檔特賣正在進行中。
　➡ In order to (commemorate / celebrate) the grand opening, our store is having its biggest sale of the year.

2 感謝您一起收聽 WTZ 電台的地方體育新聞。
　➡ Thank you for joining us on WTZ Radio for the (international / local) sports news.

3 我想可能是貴行系統把我的名字拼錯了。
　➡ I think maybe my name is (mistaken / misspelled) in your system.

4 我當時正在仔細檢閱您寄給我的銷售報告。
　➡ I was (looking after / looking over) the sales report that you sent me.

5 我想討論一項異動，這項異動將會影響到我們銀行的全體櫃員。
　➡ I would like to discuss a change that will (effect / affect) all tellers at our bank.

C 將括號內的單字按正確的順序排列組合成句子。

1 _____ slow download speeds. (than / worse / is / nothing)
　沒有什麼比下載速度緩慢更糟的了。

2 We understand _____ a new language.
　(learn / to / it / is / difficult / how)
　我們了解學習新語言有多麼困難。

3 I suggest you _____ some time outdoors.
　(enjoy / to / this / chance / take)
　我建議大家趁機到戶外走走、享受一下。

4 Let me know _____ . (when / available / are / you)
　讓我知道您何時有空。

5 _____ your monthly phone bill. (about / am / calling / I)
　我打給您，是為了您電話月租費帳單的事。

PART 4

05 發表／人物介紹

STEP 1 題型演練

A 先看題目，再聆聽獨白，並選出正確答案。 🎧 211

M Welcome, everyone, and thank you for joining me today as we celebrate the career success of our very own Justin Armil. Mr. Armil has been with our law firm for over 40 years, and he has had a great influence on everyone here during his time. Most notably, he was the founder of our community outreach program that helps needy families who are facing legal troubles. Let us all raise a glass to thank Mr. Armil and wish him happiness in his retirement.

男 歡迎大家，也感謝你們今天蒞臨，一起祝賀我們的好戰友賈斯汀‧阿爾米爾的事業成就。阿爾米爾跟我們法律事務所一同打拼超過 40 個年頭，這段期間對我們每個人都有很深的影響。最重要的是，他是我們社區擴大服務計畫的發起人，幫助了許多遇到法律糾紛的貧困家庭。讓我們舉杯感謝阿爾米爾先生，並祝福他退休後幸福快樂。

Q What is being celebrated at this event?

(A) A grand opening

(B) A new hire

(C) A retirement

(D) A product release

Q. 這場活動在慶祝什麼？

(A) 盛大開幕

(B) 新進員工

(C) 退休

(D) 產品發表

答案 (C)

▶ 本題詢問的是該活動在慶祝什麼事。獨白最後，說話者說道：「祝福他退休後幸福快樂」（wish him happiness in his retirement），表示該活動在慶祝 Mr. Armil（阿爾米爾先生）退休，因此答案為 (C)。

解題重點

- 該類型的獨白經常出現公司發生的狀況，包含與產品、銷售、培訓等有關的公開發表。
- 公開發表或人物介紹中，會出現活動獲獎者、演說者進行簡短的演說或針對人物進行介紹。
- 該類題型的題目會詢問當中提及人物的功績、產品的特點等。

B 再聽一遍上面的獨白，並針對題目選出適當的答案。 🎧 212

1 What is the purpose of this speech?

(A) To celebrate Mr. Armil's retirement

(B) To introduce a speaker

(C) To describe a program

2 What did Mr. Armil found?

(A) A shelter for needy families

(B) A program to help families in need

(C) A global company

Ⓐ 聆聽下列片語及句型，並跟著唸唸看。 🎧 213

1 發表、演說相關用語

I am here to talk about . . .
我在這裡想談……

Today, you are going to learn . . .
今天你們將學習……

Today, I want to explain . . .
今天我想說明……

We will be announcing the winners
我們即將宣布得獎者

We are pleased/delighted to announce . . .
我們很高興地宣布……

2 人物介紹相關用語

Please join me in welcoming . . .
請和我一起歡迎……

It is my pleasure to introduce . . .
我很高興介紹……

I am honored to introduce . . .
我很榮幸介紹……

He/She has been devoted to . . .
他／她為……努力付出

He/She is best known for . . .
他／她以……而聞名

He/She has been with us for（期間）
他／她跟我們一同打拼了（多長時間）

He/She has had a great influence on . . .
他／她對……有重大的影響

do an outstanding job 工作很傑出

begin his/her position as . . .
開始他／她……的職務

Ⓑ 聆聽下面的句子，並完成填空。 🎧 214

1 Today, _____ some recent changes in the employee welfare system.

   今天，我想在這裡談談員工福利制度的一些最新異動。

2 We _____ to Mr. Lee. _____ in welcoming Mr. Lee.

   我們很榮幸頒獎給李先生。請和我一起歡迎李先生。

3 She _____ for the past 30 years and has _____ the development of the company.

   她過去 30 年來跟我們公司一同打拼，為公司的發展貢獻良多。

4 _____ the employee of the year, Mr. McKinley.

   我很榮幸介紹年度最佳員工麥金利先生。

5 Ms. Robinson _____ of the training center.

   羅賓遜女士開始了她訓練中心主管的職務。

6 He _____ improving the work environment for the staff here.

   他在為本公司的員工改善工作環境一事上有重大的影響。

STEP 3 聽寫練習

Ⓐ 聆聽獨白後，針對題目選出適當的答案。 🎧215

Branch Profits

In Millions of Dollars

20
15
10
5
0

Preston   San Jose   Gutenberg   Houston
Branches

1 Look at the graphic. What branch is Ms. Spencer in charge of?

(A) Preston   (C) Gutenberg

(B) San Jose   (D) Houston

字彙 **regional** 區域的
professional knowledge 專業知識
profitable 有收益的   **encourage** 激勵
perform 表現

2 What are the listeners told to do after 12 P.M.?

(A) Sign up for a seminar

(B) Have a meal

(C) Take a photo

(D) Find a seat

字彙 **photography** 攝影   **organize** 整理
manageable 容易管理的   **pass out** 發放
make sure 確認

Ⓑ 再聽一遍獨白內容，並完成句子填空。 🎧216

1

W The next speaker I _____ is Amy Spencer, who has _____ for 10 years. _____ she joined the company in 2008, she has been _____. With her excellent _____ skills and _____, she made her branch _____ this year. That's why she is _____ her success stories and also to _____ us to _____ In our regions. I would like you to _____ a _____.

2

W _____. Please take a seat _____ _____, and we will begin. Today, _____ how to organize your photos online _____. But before we begin, _____ one detail about the conference. _____, lunch is included with the conference. _____ free lunch coupons _____, so _____ you get one before you leave. You can use it at the hotel restaurant _____.

實戰演練 Practice Test

A 聆聽下面的獨白，並選出正確答案。 🎧 217

1 Who is the speaker?

(A) A store owner

(B) A store manager

(C) A politician

(D) An investor

2 Where is the store located?

(A) In North America

(B) In Asia

(C) In Europe

(D) In Australia

3 How can visitors get a free gift?

(A) By calling a hotline

(B) By completing a survey

(C) By subscribing to a publication

(D) By recommending a friend

4 Who most likely are the listeners?

(A) Architects

(B) Lawyers

(C) Actors

(D) Police officers

5 How many awards will be announced?

(A) 3

(B) 4

(C) 5

(D) 6

6 What will most likely happen next?

(A) A meal will be served.

(B) Guests will exit the building.

(C) A movie will start.

(D) Someone will come on stage.

B 再聽一遍獨白內容，並完成句子填空。 🎧 218

[1-3]

W _____ for the grand opening of our new location! As the store manager _____ this branch of Derby's Music, let me be the first to _____. This store is our first in Europe, and I hope to _____. To start, _____ to everyone here today. All you have to do is _____. _____ on any of the tablet computers that we have _____.

[4-6]

M Good evening, everyone, and _____ the 12th annual Architecture & Construction Achievements Awards Ceremony _____ the Hong Kong Construction Initiative. _____ of the _____: Best Design, Most Practical, Most Ecofriendly, _____, and Safest. Each category _____ a committee of _____, _____, and _____. _____ of the evening is Best Design, and to announce the winner, the president of the Hong Kong Construction Initiative will be here. _____ on stage _____.

06 觀光／展覽／參觀

STEP 1 題型演練

Ⓐ 先看題目，再聆聽獨白，並選出正確答案。🎧219

M Hi. I'm Blair, and I'll be your guide on this city bus tour today. We will travel around the city and see some of the most famous and interesting sights. Unfortunately, you cannot get off the bus anytime during the tour. If you want to go back to any places to view them close up, you will have to go back after the tour ends. I strongly recommend doing so for the palace because it has a special ceremony for the changing of the guards. It's an amazing performance, and you can see it for free.

男 嗨，我是布萊爾，擔任你們今天市內觀光巴士的導遊。我們將會遊覽城市風光，參觀幾個最知名最好玩的景點。但很抱歉，在整趟旅程中，各位都不可以下車。如果您想回到任何地點就近參觀，請在行程結束之後再過去。我強烈建議大家可以在行程結束後回去參觀宮殿，那裡會舉行衛兵交接儀式，表演十分精彩，而且可以免費觀看。

Q What does the speaker recommend doing?

(A) Going to a magic performance in a park

(B) Visiting a free show at a palace

(C) Paying the cost of a tour package

(D) Checking the night scenery in a city

Q. 說話者建議做什麼？

(A) 觀賞公園的魔術表演

(B) 參觀宮殿的免費表演

(C) 花錢買套裝行程

(D) 欣賞城市夜景

答案 (B)

▶ 說話者建議導覽結束後回去觀賞衛兵交接儀式，而該活動無須支付任何費用。(B) 將文中的「ceremony performance」改寫為「free show」，故為正確答案。

🗂 解題重點

- 該類題型的內容，主要為在博物館、設施、觀光景點等地聽得到的導覽說明。
- 該類題型的題目會詢問觀光景點的相關資訊、展覽注意事項等相關細節。

Ⓑ 再聽一遍上面的獨白，並針對題目選出適當的答案。🎧220

1 Who most likely are the listeners?

(A) Clients

(B) Tourists

(C) Soldiers

2 What does the speaker say is not allowed?

(A) Eating at the palace

(B) Asking questions on the bus

(C) Getting off the bus during the tour

STEP 2　常考用法

Ⓐ 聆聽下列單字、片語及句型，並跟著唸唸看。🎧 221

① 遊覽觀光景點相關用語

tourism/tourist
觀光、旅遊／觀光客、旅客、遊客
tour guide 導遊
guided tour 導覽行程
take a look to . . . 看一下……
you will see . . . 您將看到……
head over to . . . 動身前往……
on a city bus tour 搭市內觀光巴士遊覽
bus/walking tour 巴士／徒步遊覽
establishment 店家、設施
historic building 古蹟、歷史建築
explore a city 探索城市
at the end of a tour 在導覽的尾聲
in a region 在某地區
landmark 地標
itinerary 行程
seafood market 海鮮市場
wonder of nature 大自然奇景
a species of bird 一種鳥
complimentary bottled water 附贈瓶裝水

② 博物館、參觀設施、觀看展覽相關用語

tour of a museum 博物館遊覽
newly renovated 新整修的
exhibit 展覽、展覽品
the exhibition features . . . 展覽主打……
exhibition 展覽
admission fee 入場費
free of charge 免收費
on one's way out 在某人離開時
gift shop 禮品店
souvenir 紀念品
take photographs 拍照
turn off one's camera 關掉相機
not allowed to . . . 禁止做……
not permitted 禁止（做……）
showroom 展示廳
masterpiece 傑作
donation 捐贈、捐款
wait in line 排隊
a great selection of paintings 各種精選畫作
follow me this way 跟我走這邊

Ⓑ 聆聽下面的句子，並完成填空。🎧 222

1 You ＿＿＿＿＿＿＿＿＿＿ in the museum.
　美術館內禁止拍照。

2 They will ＿＿＿ ＿＿＿＿＿ and ＿＿＿＿＿＿ next year.
　他們將重建這座古蹟，並在明年開放大眾參觀。

3 The ＿＿＿＿＿＿＿＿＿ more than 100 paintings by Picasso.
　這場現代藝術展主打百餘件的畢卡索畫作。

4 The Statue of Liberty is ＿＿＿＿＿＿＿＿＿ .
　自由女神像是紐約市的一大地標。

5 ＿＿＿＿＿＿ our next ＿＿＿＿＿＿ .
　我們出發去下一個目的地吧。

6 You can ＿＿＿＿＿＿＿＿＿ on your right.
　你可以在右側的禮品店買些紀念品。

A 聆聽獨白後，針對題目選出適當的答案。 🎧 223

1 What does the speaker say is not allowed?

(A) Feeding the animals

(B) Taking photos with a flash

(C) Entering a cave

(D) Touching bats

Van Dijk Brewery Tour	
Section 1	Beer Tasting
Section 2	Malting
Section 3	Fermenting
Section 4	Bottling & Shipping

2 Look at the graphic. Which section will the listeners go to at the end of the tour?

(A) Section 1

(B) Section 2

(C) Section 3

(D) Section 4

字彙 **cave** 洞穴 **length** 長度 **sensitive** 敏感的

字彙 **brewery** 釀酒場 **serve** 供應 **malting** 麥芽處理 **fermenting** 發酵 **bottle** 裝瓶 **ship** 裝運

B 再聽一遍獨白內容，並完成句子填空。 🎧 224

1

W All right, the _____ is going to take us into Murphy Cave. This cave system is over 150 kilometers _____, which makes it _____. It's really _____. We will only go in about 1 kilometer on today's tour. Now, there is _____ that lives here, and it is very _____. So flash photography _____ within the cave. Normal photos are fine, but you _____.

2

M Welcome to the Van Dijk Brewery tour. Let's start today with some information about the company. Did you know that Van Dijk beer _____ _____ around the world? Well, today, you are going to see _____. You will see the major processes such as malting and fermenting. You will also see _____ and _____. And _____, we will even offer you _____ three of our most _____. Follow me this way, please.

實戰演練 Practice Test

Ⓐ 聆聽下面的獨白，並選出正確答案。🎧225

1 Where is the talk taking place?

(A) On a bus

(B) In a museum

(C) In a factory

(D) In a theater

2 What is implied about the native history section?

(A) It is being renovated.

(B) It has been removed from the museum.

(C) It is free at all times.

(D) It is a private space of the building.

3 What does the speaker recommend the listeners do?

(A) Upload their photos to social media

(B) Sign up for a newsletter

(C) Exit through the garden path

(D) Visit the gift shop

4 Who most likely is the speaker?

(A) A waiter

(B) A fisherman

(C) A tour guide

(D) A show host

5 What does the speaker mean when she says, "No trip to our city is complete without a visit"?

(A) Not many people know about a place.

(B) There is a lot of competition for a place.

(C) Some people want to close an establishment.

(D) It is an essential part of the city.

6 What does the speaker say will happen tomorrow?

(A) The listeners will eat lunch at a famous restaurant.

(B) The listeners will visit the seafood market.

(C) A boat show will be at the docks.

(D) There will be a performance in a popular park.

B 再聽一遍獨白內容，並完成句子填空。 226

[1-3]

M And this _____ of the museum. Thank you all

_____, and I _____ your not being

able to see the native history section _____.

If you bring your ticket back after May 1, you can see the _____

_____ native history _____. On your way out, I

suggest _____. It has _____

and postcards. You can even mail a postcard directly from the shop _____

_____.

[4-6]

W If you all _____, _____

the Stanley Diner. Opened in 1909, this family restaurant is _____

_____ in our city. No trip to our city is _____

_____, so we are going to _____ tomorrow. For now, let's

continue our walking tour _____. There, we can learn

a bit about _____ here in Springfield and how it has

grown into the nation's _____. You will also have

about an hour of free time to _____.

07 公共場所公告／通知

STEP 1 題型演練

Ⓐ 先看題目，再聆聽獨白，並選出正確答案。🎧 227

M Attention, swimmers: The pool will be closed for the next 30 minutes for regular cleaning. Please exit the pool until the cleaning has been completed. You may still use the hot tub and spa as well as the lounge chairs. We recommend taking this chance to visit the concession stand to have a snack or to enjoy a cool drink. Thank you for your cooperation, and we hope you enjoy your time here.

男 泳客請注意：游泳池接下來將關閉 30 分鐘進行定期清潔。在清潔完成之前，請您離開游泳池。您能繼續使用熱水池、SPA 池和躺椅。我們建議您趁這個機會到販賣區享用小吃或冷飲。感謝您的配合，我們希望您在這裡玩得開心。

Q Why do the listeners have to leave the pool?

(A) It is closed for the day.

(B) Pool maintenance must be performed.

(C) There was an accident.

(D) A private party for special guests will begin.

Q. 聽眾為什麼必須離開游泳池？

(A) 今天關閉。

(B) 游泳池需要維護。

(C) 有意外發生。

(D) 特別顧客的私人聚會將開始。

答案 (B)

▶ 本題詢問聽眾必須離開游泳池的原因。前半段通知中提到「游泳池接下來將關閉 30 分鐘進行定期清潔」（The pool will be closed for the next 30 minutes for regular cleaning），因此答案為 (B)。選項將獨白中的「regular cleaning」改寫為「pool maintenance」。

📖 解題重點

- 該類題型中，會出現**商家**、**電影院**、**博物館**等公共場所內聽得到的廣播通知。
- 通知的內容包含**交通設施誤點**、**時間更動**等相關說明。
- 請務必掌握獨白中提及的地點、對象、公告或通知的目的等。

Ⓑ 再聽一遍上面的獨白，並針對題目選出適當的答案。🎧 228

1 According to the announcement, what can the listeners do while the pool is closed?

(A) Use a spa

(B) Get a massage

(C) Take a swimming lesson

2 What does the speaker recommend swimmers do?

(A) Take a break

(B) Grab a bite to eat

(C) Enjoy the hot tub

A 聆聽下列單字及片語，並跟著唸唸看。 🎧 229

1 商家、博物館相關用語

grand opening 盛大開幕（式）
shoppers/patrons 購物者／客人
grocery 雜貨
special offer 特別優惠
proceed to the register 前往收銀台
will be closed 將關門
markdown 減價
charge 收費、費用
retailer 零售業者

2 交通設施相關用語

road work 道路工程
commuter 通勤族
delay 延誤、延遲
bound for 前往……
be scheduled to 表定……、被安排……
roadside construction 路邊施工
apologize for the inconvenience
為造成不便道歉

3 展覽館、表演場地相關用語

performance/show 表演／秀
intermission 中場休息
audience 觀眾
turn off your mobile phones 將您的手機關機
prepare for the show 為表演開始做準備
refrain from taking photos 避免拍照
free of charge 免收費
appreciate your cooperation 感謝您的配合
concession stand 販賣區、販賣部

4 維護、整修相關用語

regular cleaning 定期清潔
inspection 檢查、檢驗
be temporarily closed 被暫時關閉
for safety reasons 基於安全考量
regular maintenance 定期保養
shut down （使）關閉
out of service 停止服務

B 聆聽下面的句子，並完成填空。 🎧 230

1 We are so _____ this may have caused.
對於這可能造成的任何不便，我們深感抱歉。

2 Express H1 _____ for the next couple of months.
基於安全考量，H1 快速道路接下來將關閉幾個月。

3 _____ city hall _____ soon.
往市政廳的列車很快就要來了。

4 Please make sure to _____ before the _____.
表演開始前，請確認您的手機已關機。

5 We are going to _____ with _____ for shoppers.
我們將慶祝盛大開幕，並給客人特別優惠。

6 The company gym _____.
公司健身房因為定期清潔的緣故將暫時關閉。

STEP 3 聽寫練習

A 聆聽獨白後，針對題目選出適當的答案。 🎧 231

1 According to the speaker, why will the bus be delayed?

(A) Because there is construction

(B) Because the bus left late

(C) Because there will be an unexpected stop

(D) Because they need to get more gas

> 字彙 **passenger** 乘客
> **commuter bus** 通勤巴士
> **bound for** 前往……
> **be schedule to** 表定……
> **roadside construction** 路邊施工
> **backed up** 堵車　**arrival time** 抵達時間
> **delayed** 延誤　**keep . . . in mind** 記住
> **apologize for** 為……道歉

2 Where is the announcement taking place?

(A) At a bookstore

(B) At a mall

(C) At a museum

(D) At a theater

> 字彙 **shortly** 即將　**remind** 提醒
> **refrain from** 避免做……　**cast** 演員陣容
> **free of charge** 免付費　**appreciate** 感謝
> **cooperation** 配合

B 再聽一遍獨白內容，並完成句子填空。 🎧 232

1

M Good afternoon, passengers, and welcome aboard _____ Chicago. Our trip _____ 1 hour and 30 minutes. However, _____, we expect that the roads will _____ than usual. Our _____ will likely _____ by about 30 minutes, so please _____. You can use the free Wi-Fi _____ to email or message anyone that _____ about your schedule. _____ that this delay may cause. Thank you.

2

W Ladies and gentlemen, welcome to the Fox Theater. Tonight's show, *The Story of a Boy*, _____. We would like to _____ to _____. We would also like to ask you to _____ or videos during the show. After the show, the cast will be _____ in the lobby _____. _____ and hope you enjoy the show.

A 聆聽下面的獨白，並選出正確答案。 233

1 According to the announcement, why was the schedule changed?

(A) There were too many passengers.
(B) Another flight needed to leave sooner.
(C) Some baggage has gone missing.
(D) The weather is bad.

2 What does the speaker say is available for travelers?

(A) A seat upgrade
(B) A free carry-on bag
(C) A hotel room coupon
(D) A meal

3 When can travelers leave for Moscow?

(A) Today at 9 P.M.
(B) Today at 11 P.M.
(C) Tomorrow at 11 A.M.
(D) Tomorrow at 9 P.M.

4 What does the speaker say about Pamela's Sporting Goods?

(A) It sells used sporting goods.
(B) Today is its first day of business.
(C) It has just finished some renovations.
(D) It is now under new ownership.

5 If customers buy tennis shoes, what can they get for free?

(A) Shoelaces
(B) A bag
(C) A sports towel
(D) Sports equipment

6 According to the announcement, what can customers do at the special event?

(A) Purchase a rare collector's item
(B) Receive a large discount
(C) Sign a membership contract
(D) Take a free class

B 再聽一遍獨白內容，並完成句子填空。🎧 234

[1-3]

M _____, _____. _____
caused by _____, the 9 P.M. Bard Airline flight to Moscow
_____ until tomorrow morning at 11 A.M. _____
_____ this may cause you. _____
to the nearest Bard Airline counter to _____ about
_____. _____, you can also
_____ at one of the airport hotels. Again,
_____ and thank you _____ Bard Airlines.

[4-6]

W Good evening, _____. _____
that Pamela's Sporting Goods _____ for the first time
today, and it is _____. Today only, all
customers can _____ a pair of
tennis shoes. _____, the store will be giving a free lesson on
_____ during winter. You can
find Pamela's Sporting Goods _____
of the mall.

A 選出正確的中文意思。

1　during the intermission　(A) 中場休息時　(B) 績效評估時
2　souvenir shop　(A) 館內賣場　(B) 紀念品店
3　be devoted to　(A) 期待　(B) 為……努力付出
4　subscribe to　(A) 訂閱　(B) 支援
5　outstanding ability　(A) 出色的能力　(B) 乏善可陳的能力

B 圈選出與中文意思相符的單字。

1　我很榮幸介紹本年度最佳員工。
　➡ I am (honored / pleasure) to introduce the best employee of the year.
2　艾菲爾鐵塔是法國巴黎的一大地標。
　➡ The Eiffel tower is a (skyscraper / landmark) in Paris, France.
3　這場展覽主打好幾百件知名畫家的畫作。
　➡ This exhibit (features / schedules) hundreds of paintings by famous painters.
4　請享用您飯店客房附贈的瓶裝水。
　➡ Enjoy the (available / complimentary) bottled water in your hotel room.
5　她對改善臨時工權利一事的影響深遠。
　➡ She has had a great (significance / influence) on improving the rights of part-time workers.

C 將括號內的單字按正確的順序排列組合成句子。

1　We ＿＿＿＿＿＿＿＿＿＿＿＿ and hope you have a good time.
　(truly / your / appreciate / cooperation)
　我們誠摯感謝您的配合，並祝您玩得愉快。
2　He ＿＿＿＿＿＿＿＿＿＿ for the last 20 years.
　(has / with / been / the company)
　他過去 20 年來都跟公司一同打拼。
3　＿＿＿＿＿＿＿＿＿＿ will be arriving shortly. (bound / the train / for / Oxford)
　開往牛津的火車即將抵達。
4　This tour ＿＿＿＿＿＿＿＿＿＿ two and a half hours.
　(is / scheduled / take / to)
　這個行程表定將花費兩個半小時。
5　You are not ＿＿＿＿＿＿＿＿＿＿ in the museum.
　(to / take / allowed / photographs)
　博物館內禁止拍照。

Half Test

LISTENING TEST 🎧235

In the Listening test, you will be asked to demonstrate how well you understand spoken English. The entire Listening test will last approximately 20 minutes. There are four parts, and directions are given for each part. You must mark your answers on the separate answer sheet. Do not write your answers in your test book.

PART 1

Directions: For each question in this part, you will hear four statements about a picture in your test book. When you hear the statements, you must select the one statement that best describes what you see in the picture. Then find the number of the question on your answer sheet and mark your answer. The statements will not be printed in your test book and will be spoken only one time.

Statement (D), "She is ironing a garment," is the best description of the picture, so you should select answer (D) and mark it on your answer sheet.

1.

2.

GO ON TO THE NEXT PAGE

3.

PART 2 🎧236

Directions: You will hear a question or statement and three responses spoken in English. They will not be printed in your test book and will be spoken only one time. Select the best response to the question or statement and mark the letter (A), (B), or (C) on your answer sheet.

4. Mark your answer on your answer sheet.

5. Mark your answer on your answer sheet.

6. Mark your answer on your answer sheet.

7. Mark your answer on your answer sheet.

8. Mark your answer on your answer sheet.

9. Mark your answer on your answer sheet.

10. Mark your answer on your answer sheet.

11. Mark your answer on your answer sheet.

12. Mark your answer on your answer sheet.

13. Mark your answer on your answer sheet.

14. Mark your answer on your answer sheet.

15. Mark your answer on your answer sheet.

16. Mark your answer on your answer sheet.

17. Mark your answer on your answer sheet.

PART 3 🎧 237

Directions: You will hear some conversations between two or more people. You will be asked to answer three questions about what the speakers say in each conversation. Select the best response to each question and mark the letter (A), (B), (C), or (D) on your answer sheet. The conversations will not be printed in your test book and will be spoken only one time.

18. Why does the woman want to meet the man?

(A) To discuss their new product
(B) To arrange a meeting time
(C) To launch a new product
(D) To prepare for a business trip

19. When are the speakers going to meet?

(A) On Monday
(B) On Tuesday
(C) On Wednesday
(D) On Thursday

20. What does the man say he will do?

(A) Reserve a flight ticket
(B) Send a car to the woman
(C) Call the director of Manufacturing
(D) Make a schedule for next week

21. Who most likely is the woman?

(A) A hotel clerk
(B) A store manager
(C) A technician
(D) A hotel guest

22. What problem is being discussed?

(A) A shower is broken.
(B) There is no warm water.
(C) A room is too noisy.
(D) There are too many guests on the floor.

23. What is the man advised to do?

(A) Enjoy the swimming pool
(B) Take a break
(C) Use a shower by the pool
(D) Check out immediately

GO ON TO THE NEXT PAGE ▶

24. Where does the conversation most likely take place?

(A) In a meeting room
(B) At a hotel
(C) At a convention center
(D) In an auditorium

25. What does the man imply when he says, "I think that worked out very well"?

(A) Some planning turned out to be effortless.
(B) A previous event was successful.
(C) They found a good location for an upcoming event.
(D) The office renovations were ahead of schedule.

26. What will the man probably do next?

(A) Call for a meeting to discuss an event
(B) Cancel their reservation at the city convention center
(C) Confirm a reservation at the Terrace Hotel
(D) Contact a convention center about an event

----

27. What is the conversation mostly about?

(A) Conducting an interview
(B) Revising company policies
(C) Offering a person full-time employment
(D) Arranging a business trip

28. What does the woman say about Lena?

(A) She is not punctual.
(B) Her performance has been great.
(C) She gets along well with her coworkers.
(D) She is not interested in the job.

29. How will the man contact Lena?

(A) By email
(B) By letter
(C) By phone
(D) In person

Shuttle Names	Destinations	Operating Hours
Blue	Amusement Park	Every 30 minutes
Red	Big C Shopping Mall	Every 60 minutes
Yellow	Train Station	Every 30 minutes
Green	Big C Shopping Mall	Every 20 minutes

30. What does the woman ask the man for?

(A) The best way to get to the shopping mall

(B) The best way to avoid traffic

(C) How to make a reservation for the shuttle service

(D) How to save money on transportation costs

31. Why does the man say a taxi is not a good option?

(A) Because it is usually pricy

(B) Because there is a lot of traffic now

(C) Because it does not come to the building where she is

(D) Because the pickup time is not guaranteed

32. Look at the graphic. Which shuttle bus will the woman probably take?

(A) Blue

(B) Red

(C) Yellow

(D) Green

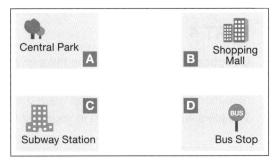

33. What are the speakers mainly discussing?

(A) Where to stay during their trip

(B) Where to go for vacation

(C) What to do during their vacation

(D) How to get to Buenos Aires

34. What did the man say about their previous trip?

(A) The food was awful.

(B) It was hard to get around.

(C) It was too crowded.

(D) The shopping mall was far away.

35. Look at the graphic. Where will the speakers probably stay?

(A) A

(B) B

(C) C

(D) D

GO ON TO THE NEXT PAGE ▶

PART 4 🎧 238

Directions: You will hear some talks given by a single speaker. You will be asked to answer three questions about what the speaker says in each talk. Select the best response to each question and mark the letter (A), (B), (C), or (D) on your answer sheet. The talks will not be printed in your test book and will be spoken only one time.

36. Who is the speaker?

    (A) The owner of Good Beats

    (B) The organizer of an event

    (C) A product designer

    (D) A product manager

37. What product is being discussed?

    (A) Headphones

    (B) A mobile phone

    (C) A computer game

    (D) A fitness tracker

38. What is special about the product?

    (A) It is good for the price.

    (B) It is waterproof.

    (C) It has additional new features.

    (D) It comes with a free extended warranty.

39. According to the speaker, what happened recently?

    (A) An IT conference was held.

    (B) Some policies were changed.

    (C) A new technician was hired.

    (D) Some software was installed.

40. What was Jeremy asked to do?

    (A) Delete some old software

    (B) Provide software training

    (C) Purchase some new software

    (D) Stay in the office for a while

41. What are the listeners advised to do?

    (A) Register for a training session

    (B) Ask Jeremy for help in person

    (C) Install some new software

    (D) Attend an IT seminar

42. What is the talk mainly about?

(A) Next year's budget
(B) An upcoming move
(C) Public transportation
(D) A new company policy

43. What does the speaker imply when she says, "I think this is the right decision"?

(A) The new promotion was successful.
(B) The new location is convenient.
(C) Hiring more staff was a good choice.
(D) The company paid less money for the office.

44. What will the speaker probably do next?

(A) Discuss some ways to save money
(B) Share ideas on how to promote sales
(C) Give details about the new location
(D) Review a budget proposal

- -

45. Where does the announcement most likely take place?

(A) At a library
(B) At a gym
(C) At a store
(D) At a lottery shop

46. What is the speaker announcing?

(A) A grand opening
(B) An upcoming renovation
(C) A clearance sale
(D) A celebratory event

47. What can a person win in the lucky drawing?

(A) A 50% discount
(B) Airline tickets
(C) A cash prize
(D) A free snack

- -

Billy's Office Furniture
179 Broadway

May, 10

Item	Quantity	Unit Price
Chair	2 units	$45
Table	1 unit	$70
Cabinet	1 unit	$120

Total: $280

---

48. What is the purpose of the call?

(A) To inform the listener that an ordered item is not in stock
(B) To place an order for additional chairs
(C) To give information about an ongoing sale
(D) To say that there is a problem with a receipt

49. What information is Mr. Parker asked to provide?

(A) An order number
(B) Credit card information
(C) A proof of purchase
(D) Contact details

50. Look at the graphic. How much money will be returned to the listener?

(A) 45 dollars
(B) 70 dollars
(C) 90 dollars
(D) 120 dollars

This is the end of the Listening test.